STEPBROTHER, PLEASE STOP TEASING ME!

Volume Thirteen

MIA CLARK

Cherrylily

This is a work of fiction. Similarities to real people, places, or events are
entirely coincidental.

Stepbrother, Please Stop Teasing Me!
(Volume Thirteen)

Copyright © 2023 Mia Clark

Written by Mia Clark

CONTENTS

ABOUT THE BOOK

Shy good girl Charlotte Scott is secretly dating her new stepbrother, Hunter Jackson.

This was actually going quite well until Hunter's evil ex-girlfriend found out and decided to:

- A.) Challenge her to an amateur night pole dancing competition
- B.) Demand she back down from being both Hunter's stepsister *and* his girlfriend if she loses
- C.) Be really mean to everyone for no real reason
- D.) All of the above

(P.S. ~ It's D, but they're all kind of tied together, aren't they?)
Anyways, tonight's the night!

Charlotte will do anything and everything it takes to prove to herself and to Hunter that she'll fight for him no matter what.

…Even if it means seductively dancing on a pole in front of a live audience.

(And Hunter. He'll be there. It's honestly mostly for him.)
She may not have thought this through very well…

(VALENTINE'S DAY SPECIAL) ROSE PETAL RUMORS

Episode 162

~*~ *Valentine's Day Special* ~*~

CHARLOTTE

"**A**lright, babes, look," Angela says, tough and determined. "If we're doing this, we need to do it *together*. It totally won't work any other way. Understand? We need to form a unified front and stand tall in the face of adversity or else it's just never going to happen. Are we all in agreement here?"

"Um, can I ask a quick question first?" I ask, because something's been nagging at the back of my mind and I really feel like I need to point it out before this goes too far.

"Yes, Charlie, babe, always," Angela says, as if I'm clearly an authority figure on this particular subject. "What's going on in that pretty little head of yours?"

"I..." I start to say, pausing immediately. I just, um... I feel like if I say this it might cause issues and I don't want to upset anyone but also... "Do we actually *need* to do this? I don't really get it."

I'm in the middle of a very pink meeting in the

cheerleader locker room. It's not just a cheer squad meeting, though. Oh no. This is a meeting to determine the future Valentine's Day plans of the entire school, potentially forever. It involves spreading rumors, sticking to our feminine values, understanding our worth as women, and, um... Angela explained it a lot better and it sounded really good at the time and all the cheerleaders agreed vehemently, cheering uproariously immediately after she finished explaining her rosy scheme.

Anyways, the cheerleaders stare at me, wide-eyed, as if, um... Angela and I are about to fight it out for dominance leadership of the cheer squad and this battle will determine who's in charge from here on out.

...I don't want to fight anyone and I hope it's just the way they look right now but I'm still super confused...

"Babe, no," Angela says, shaking her head, sighing. "We need to do this. If we don't, what do you think will happen?"

"...Nothing?" I offer.

"Babe! For real! You don't seem to understand how important this is for our future. If we don't take a stand now, what then? Who will stand up for us when we need it most?"

"Look," Portia says. "I was onboard with the idea at first since the entire squad was agreeing to it, but actually since Charlie spoke up and, you know, voiced exactly what I was thinking... come on, Angela. Is this *really* necessary?"

"It is," Angela says. "I get it, alright? You may not think it's important now. It might not even be that important this year. But one year, sometime in the distant future, every girl who attends college here will thank us. And we'll thank *ourselves*, babes. We *deserve* this. Do we not? If any single one of you actually thinks otherwise, please, speak up! But you all know, deep down in your V-Day hearts, this is something we owe it to ourselves to do, for our sexy future selves, for the cute and innocent little freshman that'll hallow these halls next year, the year after that, and every single year until the end of the world. That's how important this is, babes. Totally."

I mean, when she says it like that...

"Okay," I say, signing on. "I... I didn't mean to, um... dissent for no reason, so... I think it's good now?"

"Thanks, Charlie!" Angela says, leaning close to hug me sideways. "Love you, babe! But seriously, this'll be a good thing, okay?"

I nod and nod and, um... I nod again just in case.

"Are you in or are you out, Portia?" Angela asks one last time.

Portia's eyes dart back and forth as she realizes the entirety of the cheer squad is staring at her now, waiting for her answer to see the strength of her resolve. It's impressive and also intimidating.

"Fine," she begrudgingly agrees. "I'll do it, but if this ruins my V-Day plans... for real, I'm going to be upset, ladies."

"It won't," Angela says, fully believing in her abilities. "Trust me, babe. It's absolutely perfect. Nothing could possibly go wrong."

That's, um... yes... okay then...

HUNTER

Me and the boys are getting dressed after football practice when suddenly everyone on the team circles around us, staring at me in particular, waiting for me to, uh... I don't actually know what the fuck the problem is?

"What?" I ask, furrowing my brow and asking this impromptu gathering as a whole what's up.

"Have you heard, Jacksy?" Damian asks.

"Why do they even want us to do that?" Fred adds.

"Beats me," Johan says with a shrug. "I thought the entire point was just a casual now and then thing, right? Girls are weird, man."

"Okay, so," I say, starting with the only thing I understand out of any of that. "Girls *are* fucking weird," I say in full agreement. "But why are they weird this time?"

"Oh, I heard about this!" Teddy says, eager to include himself. "I didn't think it was that bad?"

"Are you insane?" Oliver asks, completely disagreeing. "Dude, it's fucking bad."

"I didn't think it was that bad either," Sam says with a shrug. "I'm fine with it."

"Guys," I say, panicking slightly. "Fuck. What is it? What the hell's going on and why is it bad or not bad?"

"The cheerleaders started it," Damian says. "I think. That's the rumor, at least."

"I heard it started with cheerleaders from a different school," Johan adds.

"The way it was told to me, it's an ancient tradition that apparently needs to be followed or else something really fucking bad happens," Fred says. "Like, *really* bad, dudes. I'm talking, uh... I don't know, but what're we thinking, boys?"

This starts an uproar of continued rumors I've never heard before, including:

"I heard you can never get an erection again if you don't do it."

"I heard your dick falls off completely. You keep your balls, though."

"I heard if you *don't* do it the next girl you sleep with is guaranteed to get pregnant."

"What if you want to get them pregnant, though?"

"I mean, in that case they don't, right? It's something bad, not good. That's how it works."

They start fighting it out, arguing with each other about what is and isn't bad, how it happens, what the rules and requirements are, and... holy fucking shit just shut up for a goddamn second, you assholes.

"Quiet!" I shout, jumping onto one of the benches in the

football locker room. The guys focus on me, so that's good. "Can somebody explain to me what the fuck is happening and why you're all freaking out?"

Everyone starts mumbling and apologizing but nobody wants to say what the rumor is. Which leads me to believe it's dumb as fuck and they're being idiots. But for the sake of helping the dudes out, I turn to Teddy for assistance.

"Teddy, you're up. Why's everyone panicking? What's up, bro?"

"Am I supposed to stand on the bench to say it or should I stay down here?" he asks.

I shrug. "Doesn't really matter. You want to come up here, man?"

"Sure, might be easier."

I hold my hand out and help Teddy up and he nods and thanks me and turns to the panic-stricken crowd of football players surrounding us.

"So," Teddy says, starting strong. "Rumor has it the girls are calling for a booty call embargo this year for Valentine's Day. There will be no booty calls. I repeat, none! That's everything from casual flings to friends with benefits and even if you're dating someone and it's not actually a booty call, per se, but, like, you want to make love on Valentine's Day? The girls say it's not allowed unless the boy involved scatters rose petals on the bed first. Oh, it has to involve a bed, too. I was talking to Angela about it and she said there can't be any loopholes. All the girls have agreed to this. Apparently it'll be strictly enforced."

"Uhhhhh..." I grunt, because I don't know what to say now. "Wait, is that it?"

"Is that fucking it?" Damian counters. "*Dude!*"

"It means we won't get laid for Valentine's Day," Johan adds.

"We can't even attempt a poophole loophole," Fred says. "I asked."

"It's called anal sex, you fucking idiot," I snap. "Seriously, never say that shit again. It's banned. Forever."

"Whatever, dude, I just thought it sounded funny and I was trying to lighten the mood. No need to be a dick about it."

"Anyways, guys, come on. What's the big deal? If you want to get laid on Valentine's Day, buy some roses or whatever, sprinkle the petals on a bed, and go to town."

Seriously, I kind of thought this was obvious, no loopholes needed, but they start looking at me like I'm insane and I don't even know why.

"You don't understand," Olly says, siding with the others. "That's way too fucking romantic, Jacksy. And what happens next? Your fuck buddy wants you to take her out on dates?"

"...I'm not seeing the issue there either?" I reply.

"What if we don't want to screw in a bed?" Damian points out. "What then?"

"No offense, but I don't think it'll kill you to have sex with your girl in a bed on Valentine's Day," I tell him. "It's really not a big deal."

"It's the principle of the matter, man. The goddamn principle."

"Okay, look. Here. You want a fucking loophole? I have one for you. If you want to have sex standing up, doggystyle, or whatever the fuck, spread some goddamn rose petals on a bed and do it there. No one said you have to do it missionary."

This elicits a bunch of *oohs* and *ahhs* as if I'm a genius somehow and it's very fucking strange because I've never felt like that once in my entire life. Now, though? Maybe.

"Isn't that dangerous?" Teddy asks. "I don't think it's a good idea to have sex while standing up in a bed. You might fall."

"Alright, I kind of get it if you're standing in the middle of the bed, but think outside the box, buddy," I answer. "If you're standing at the head of the bed and she's facing the wall with her hands against it and you're right behind her... there you go. Easy."

"That seems a little better but there could still be balancing issues and I wouldn't want anyone to get hurt, you know?"

"Exactly! Teddy understands!" Fred cries out. "Missionary sex sucks balls!"

"Hey, go fuck yourself," I shout. "Missionary's great. You can grab your girl's ass and pull her against you while you thrust in deep and it's fucking hot as hell and intimate and feels goddamn amazing. Don't say stupid shit like that ever again. I swear to God, you're all being little babies about nothing."

"I get it, Jacksy," Olly says, sighing and shaking his head. "I would've agreed with you at one point, too. But it's different for the rest of us, man. You have a girlfriend, so to you it's not a big deal. To us, though? If we start treating our casual, no strings attached, booty call fuck buddies with benefits with romantic bullshit like rose petal booty calls, well... it starts with Valentine's Day but where does it end? Next thing you know they're going to want it all the time. Every night of hardcore casual fuck sessions will have to be intimate and romantic. And you know what? It's not casual at that point. It's dating. They're trying to lure us into relationships and make us treat them like girlfriends. And I, for one, uh... I'm not actually against it because I'm kind of gunning for Hannah and if I can swing it I'll totally impress her with rose petals in bed, but we aren't anywhere close to that so I'm going stag for this one. For the rest of the team, though? Solidarity, man."

"Thanks, Olly," Johan says.

"You're the best, man!" Fred agrees.

Damian steps forward, bro fisting it up with Oliver. "Solidarity, buddy."

It's at this point I realize there's one thing and one thing only I can do. It's drastic and I usually wouldn't use it as a first line of offense, but everyone's riled up and worried and I think it's for the best.

And so...

"Teddy," I say, nodding to my best bud. "Please explain to these assholes why what Olly just said is stupid as fuck. Thanks."

"Uh, sure?" Teddy says. "How long do I have?"

"Can I leave?" Sam asks. "I already know the answer and I told Amelia I'd paint miniatures with her after practice."

"Huh? What the hell is that?" I ask.

"I thought it was weird at first but it's pretty cool," Sam says, excited. "She buys unpainted polyurethane resin miniature figurines from this local game shop. It's to do with the *Caverns & Dragons* game, right? So some of them are humans or whatever, like rogues, druids, stuff like that. Some are dragons or monsters or goblins or they even have bigger ones like houses sometimes but she isn't into those. Anyways, Amelia buys a couple new ones every so often and she has a special paint set with tiny brushes and she paints them herself and Tania uses them when we play at lunch sometimes. Today I'm painting a goblin rogue chick with massive tits."

"I really wish I could say that's dumb but it sounds kind of cool. You got any pics, bro?"

"Of the goblin rogue chick with massive tits or just whatever?"

"I mean, either one works."

Sam whips out his phone and shows me a picture of a miniature figurine of a goblin rogue chick with massive tits and, you know, she does indeed have massive tits. Like, no offense, but rogues are supposed to be sneaky as hell, right? How's this girl sneaking around with those? They're barely contained in her shirt. I don't fucking get it. Magic's definitely involved. I guess that's the name of the game, though. They do magic bullshit all the time, so this is just another example of the power of spells or something.

Anyways, while Sam and I check out photos of miniatures online, Teddy explains what the issue is to the rest of the guys.

"Even if it's a casual fling, it's good to treat your partner with respect and love," Teddy says. "There's a big difference between being *in* love and treating someone *with* love, you know? Like, I think we can all agree if you're having a one night stand with a girl then you want to make sure you're nice to her, right?"

"Okay, Teddy, I kind of get you and I know where you're going with this, but what if in the middle of banging it out the girl says something like, *'Yes, choke me, Daddy!'* you know? What then?"

"I don't think it's a good idea to do things without talking about it first, so that's probably something that should come up before your clothes come off, but there's safe ways to hold a girl's throat that kind of feels like choking but it's not actually dangerous? It's just something to be cautious of, that's all. But maybe she should mention she wants to call you Daddy beforehand, too? I don't know, guys. It's not my thing and I don't think I'd like it if that happened to me."

"Fair enough, man. I don't hate it and sometimes I'm kind of into it but it depends on the girl, you know? I was more asking if that's considered nice. Because I don't think choking someone is nice?"

"If it's consensual then it's okay," Teddy says with a nod. "It's, like... there's three things to keep in mind, alright? Before you engage in anything sexual, you need to ask yourself these questions: Is it safe, sane, and consensual? If the answer is yes to all three, you're good to go."

"Damn, bro. That's really useful. Thanks!"

"Okay, but also, to continue on, I think the issue at hand here is, uh... you're worried the girls will want a more serious relationship if you include rose petals in a casual fling, right? Except I think you should treat them nicely even if it's casual. Like, everyone deserves respect, guys. Even if it's casual and maybe *especially* if it's casual. There's this, uh... I mean this is going to sound kind of silly but my dad taught it to me when I was younger and I think about it sometimes. Basically there's campground rules, right?"

"I've never been camping," Johan says. "Am I missing out?"

"Fuck yeah you're missing out," Damian says. "Camping's the best. You feel like you're at one with your inner self and you get to walk around shirtless and sit by a fire. Cool as hell."

"Just bring bug spray," Teddy adds. "Anyways, uh... so when you go camping, campground rules state you should leave the campsite better off than when you left it, right? Meaning you should clean up after yourself and honor and respect nature because it's the right thing to do. So I think it's good to have the same philosophy when you have any kind of relationship with a girl, too?"

"So you're saying if I blow my load all over her tits I should clean her up after?" Fred offers, sincere as fuck.

"...Maybe? I mean, that *is* a pretty nice thing to do. I was more talking about how you should leave the girl better off than she was before. Honor and respect her, even if it's only a casual one night thing. Because it's the right thing to do."

"I get it," Damian says, excited. "Like if she stays the night, instead of making an excuse to kick her out of bed as soon as possible, maybe ask if she wants to grab breakfast?"

Teddy nods, excited. "Exactly! It's just breakfast, dudes. You don't have to see her again after that if you don't want to."

"What if *she* wants to, though?" Johan asks. "What then?"

"I mean... if that happens, maybe consider if you want to see her again and go from there? If not, just tell her it was fun and you had a good time but you aren't looking for anything serious and you don't want to hurt her feelings if she's looking for a relationship."

I vaguely heard most of that but Sam keeps showing me these cool as hell miniature figurines and I'm kind of into them now. The most recent one is a dark elf warrior wielding a massive fucking sword bigger than his entire body. I don't think he could actually ever swing it around, but it's fantasy so whatever. Looks amazing and if I had any idea how to paint it I'd definitely want to.

Anyways, yeah--

"Are we good now?" I ask, just kind of hoping that's it and Teddy's done explaining everything.

"I think so?" Teddy says, but I don't like the way he says it.

"Maybe we *should* be doing more for the girls?" Johan asks, positing the question to the rest of the bros. "I enjoy going to breakfast as much as anyone, you know?"

"What if we ask them if they want to go to breakfast and they give us a weird look, though?" Damian counters. "What then?"

"I'll go to breakfast with you anytime, man," Fred says, patting him on the back. "It's cool."

"Thanks, dude."

I think that's it and everyone else agrees and, uh... while they're chatting about this and that, rose petals and breakfast and other weird shit I don't understand because I was looking at miniatures with Sam while Teddy apparently said way more than I expected...

"You know what this means now?" Olly asks as we leave the locker room, leaving Sam to his miniature painting and Teddy to further explain whatever it is he needs to explain.

"Uh, no?" I ask. "What?"

Olly grins, mischievous. "I don't actually know but I'm going to enjoy watching it happen."

Whatever, bro. I'm sure everything's fine.

CHARLOTTE

I'm sitting in the cafeteria with Angela, Jenny, and Clarissa when suddenly Portia shrieks at us, or, um... it's mostly at Angela but I'm right across the table from her and I feel like it's at me, too?

"*Angela!*" Portia wails. "What the hell have you done?!"

This is followed by Portia loudly stomping across the cafeteria to confront the head cheerleader. Portia poutily smacks her hand against the tabletop, but she does it a little too hard and pouts more, looking at her red hand after.

"Ow," she grumbles. "That hurt."

"Babe, like, be careful please!" Angela says.

"But seriously," Portia says, going back to it. "You said this was just about rose petals but why is Johan saying if we hook up again this year he wants to have a talk about the choking thing I like and he's not into being called Daddy so maybe we can think of something else that's hot and sexy to use for dirty talk instead? He even mentioned going to *breakfast* the next morning if I wanted to sleep over. Which, like, don't get me wrong, I love breakfast. But it's weird. It's freaking weird, Angela! We've *never* gone to breakfast before and I don't know how I feel about any of this."

I understood half of that and I, um... I'm trying to help, so...

"Maybe he's, um... he's not ready to have a baby?" I offer.

Portia stares at me like I have eight heads and they all look a little funny. I only have one head and maybe it looks funny but I kind of like it so I don't know?

"It's because Portia has daddy issues," Clarissa informs me. "She likes calling boys Daddy in bed. It's kind of her thing? Along with the whole wearing skimpy clothes thing. She has a lot of things and they aren't for everyone but we totally support her!"

"...Thanks for that, Clarissa," Portia says, deadpan. "I don't even have daddy issues, though! I just thought boys were into it, you know?"

"Maybe try Papi instead?" Clarissa offers.

"*Mon pere?*" Jenny adds. "Switch it up now and then. Use a different language. Keep him on his toes."

"I don't know if anyone should be choking anyone, either?" I add, just in case everyone forgot that part. "It seems dangerous?"

"So, like, I get that, and I totally understand where you're coming from, Charlie," Portia says, informative. "But it's not that I actually want to be choked and more like I enjoy the feeling of a man's hand around my throat? If he lightly pushes his fingers against the side of my neck so it's just a little pressure and not a full on choke, I can still breathe fine and, um... it just really does it for me, you know?"

"It *is* really fun..." Clarissa says, wistful. "I don't even know why? It just is."

"Like, totally, babes," Angela agrees with a nod. "But, on the other hand... not all boys are the forceful and dominating types, am I right? Some are more soft and gentle and that's really fun every now and then and I don't think we should be upset if they don't want to lightly choke us every now and then. It's the same as if we don't want to do anal, you know?"

"I *do* want to do anal, though," Portia says, confused. "I don't get it?"

"Portia, babe, it's not about if you do or don't, but everyone has their limits, babe. That's what I meant."

"Breakfast is my hard limit," Portia says. "I'm not going to breakfast with Damian after screwing his brains out on V-Day! It's bad enough I have to do the rose petal thing. What if I want him to rail me from behind while I'm pinned against the wall, Angela? Your plan is bad. You should feel bad for making us follow this stupid plan!"

"It's not a stupid plan!" Clarissa snaps. "You take that back!"

The cheerleaders start to argue and I don't know what to do and Jenny looks really entertained the whole time, just quietly nibbling on french fry after french fry. I think the entire cafeteria is watching us now and, um... that's a bit awkward but they're mostly watching Portia and Clarissa so it's not as bad as if they were watching me, and...

"Babes, as much as I want to have this conversation, now isn't the time nor the place, you know?" Angela says after the heated discussion dies down slightly. "What's wrong with breakfast anyways? I think breakfast sounds nice!"

"Well, it's not!" Portia proclaims. "It's the principle of it, Angela. It's, like, first I agree to have breakfast with him, then I'm meeting his parents, and what next? I'm sitting next to his toothless grandpa at Thanksgiving? Um, no. Never! I refuse!"

...I don't actually know what's wrong with any of those things and I don't get to ask because shortly after saying all that Portia stomps off as quickly as she stormed in and the cafeteria is mostly quiet again save for a few interested rumblings echoing around the rest of the tables...

"Do you think maybe we did something bad on accident?" Clarissa asks Angela.

"Babe, no," Angela says, staunchly supporting her plan. "Nobody said it'd be easy. It's hard, babes. It totally is. But the payoff is worth it. I promise."

"At the very least, it's fun watching everyone get upset about it," Jenny says with a smirk. "Never thought I'd see anyone get mad about a guy she slept with wanting to take her to breakfast..."

"I mean, it depends where he wants to go, right?" Clarissa asks. "What if it's McReynold's?"

"They have good hashbrowns?" I say. "Um... I like to... to buy a hashbrown and a breakfast sandwich and... and you put the hashbrown *inside* the breakfast sandwich and, um..."

"Charlie," Clarissa says, gaping at me. "Oh my gosh that sounds amazing!"

"It *does* sound amazing," Angela agrees. "But, like, babe, do you know how many carbs that is?"

"What if the boy you slept with pays for it, though?" Jenny asks.

"It's still carbs, babe."

"Is it okay if it's for V-Day, though?" Clarissa asks, hopeful. "Like... just once a year is totally fine, right?"

"*Babe...*" Angela says, sighing and shaking her head, except at the last second she relents. "Alright, fine. It's okay for V-Day. That's it, though!"

"Yay!"

"Do, um... do you all want to go to breakfast at McReynold's for Valentine's Day?" I ask, because I'm kind of excited now.

"Yes, please! Let's go, Charlie! I'm so excited now."

"That was supposed to be a treat for sticking to the rose petal booty call rule," Angela huffs. "Ugh. Fine! Yes, let's totally do breakfast, babes. But don't forget the rest of the rules!"

(VALENTINE'S DAY SPECIAL) CREATIVE THINKING

Episode 163

HUNTER

I don't know what happened or when it happened, but the entire school's gone crazy for Valentine's Day.

I'm sitting with the guys in our only class we have together. Class hasn't started yet and the professor isn't here, so...

"I usually go with the Valentine's and chill approach," this guy in the back says. "But since the girls want rose petals because of that rumor, I figure a candlelit coffee at Starbricks first and a walk around campus, followed by snacks, a steamy Netflix movie playing in the background, then I haul out the rose petals, scatter those fuckers on the bed while she's laying down, and... *bam!*"

"It's kind of fun, right?" another guy adds. "I used to think there was a lot of pressure to be as casual as possible but after a hookup I like cuddling a little, you know? It's nice knowing the girls won't take it seriously and we can still be friends with benefits after."

"Do you think it's best to buy roses, give them to her, and *then* pluck the petals later and scatter them on the bed? Or should we buy roses specifically for the bed and separate roses for her?"

"Is this only for straight couples? I don't want anything bad happening. For gay couples, who needs to do the rose petal thing?"

"I asked Alice since she knows Angela who first heard about the rose petal rumor, right? She said it doesn't matter what your sexual orientation is, one of you has to get the petals. It's mandatory no matter what. Make sure everyone knows. I wouldn't want something bad to happen to anyone on accident."

And on and on and on and... holy fucking shit...

I stare at Oliver who looks incredibly fucking pleased with himself, as if he knew this was going to happen and he's loving the ensuing chaos. Teddy and Sam seem oblivious. I don't get it, man.

Like, seriously... nothing bad's going to happen! Also, why's everyone overthinking it? I'm not saying rose petals are a bad thing to toss around before a booty call, but this is getting a little extreme, don't you think?

"So..." Sam says, smirking at me. "You get rose petals for Charlie yet?"

"...No?" I answer.

"Jacksy's going against the grain, guys," Olly says, snickering. "He's the only guy on campus who doesn't plan on getting laid for V-Day."

"Look, asshole," I snap. "Whether I do or don't plan on getting laid is none of your business, so..."

"The flowers you got for Baby Charlie were really nice, Jacksy," Teddy says. "Great job."

"Thanks, Teddy," I say, both appreciative and also, uh... "How'd you know I got her flowers?"

"Jenny texted me a picture. She said the flowers were super cute and why didn't I get her flowers like I used to?"

"You used to buy your sister flowers?" Olly asks, staring at him. "Uh, why?"

"It's just a nice thing to do? Remember when we were in elementary school and we'd give our friends chocolates and cards. Same thing. You don't just have to get your girlfriend something for Valentine's Day, Olly."

"Ah, the good old days..." Sam says, sighing wistfully. "I used to cause so much drama. I'd slip a note in every girl's locker saying I was their secret admirer. Sometimes with chocolates, sometimes flowers, and I'd watch them try to figure out who did it. Eventually I did it openly and watched them stare at me in class trying to figure out if I was into them or if I was just being nice. Those were the days, boys."

"So basically the exact same thing you do now?" I say. "Got it."

"I mean, yeah, I flirt it up a lot, but it's college, man. It's expected, right?"

"What'd you get Amelia, though?" Olly asks, curious.

"I got her pink roses. She nearly died and then ran off."

"...Yeah?"

"It was great."

"Look, who cares?" I say, trying to get back to whatever the hell's going on. "I got Baby Sis flowers, we're hanging out later, and if things go further, I doubt the fact that I'm not scattering rose petals on a bed will make anything bad happen, so..."

"While I fully agree, and I don't want to take away from your attempt at bucking the trend, the girls have a solidarity pact. They're refusing to have sex unless rose petals are involved."

I stare at Sam, because I'm pretty sure he's fucking with me. Olly smirks, indicating Sam may not be fucking with me. Teddy shrugs, apologetic, and it's at that point I realize no one is fucking with me and it's all true.

"No fucking way," I say.

...Where the hell do I get rose petals on Valentine's Day?

Seriously, everywhere's sold out. No roses whatsoever. It's Valentine's Day, man. Everyone bought them. Especially this year since people are going crazy over the fact they *need* rose petals to get laid.

I was fine a few minutes ago and now I'm freaking out because there's no fucking way I'm not making love to Baby Sis on Valentine's Day. If there's a day to do it, it's today. I had plans. I had ideas. I had, uh... I mean, the plans weren't that detailed and the ideas were vague thoughts about how romantically as fuck I was going to seduce the hell out of her. But it's all for naught because I don't have rose petals?

I flat out fucking refuse to accept this, and so--

I text my stepsister quick just in case, because I need an answer as soon as possible:

> "Yo, dude, is it true we can't have sex without rose petals?"

Her reply?

BABY SIS

> "That's the most romantic thing anyone's ever said to me."

She also adds:

"I'm kidding. Was that funny? Sorry! I thought it was a good joke. I told Angela I'd go along with the rest of the girls but we don't have to do it today if you don't want? I can wait! I don't know if I want to wait. I've never done it on Valentine's Day. Is it different? Everyone seems excited and I don't fully understand but maybe it's just really good today and if we don't do it I'll be missing out and I don't want to miss out but there's no pressure either so whatever you want to do is fine. Okay I typed way too much and I don't think I can delete it now so I'm hitting send. I hope this isn't too much. Bye."

So... that was a lot, but also, fuck. I text her back.

"Where are you? We need to talk. This is dire. For real. I think I fucked up."

"Oh no. I'm in the art club room. Do you want to come here?"

I don't answer. No time. Shit's going down and I can't waste a second. I lunge out of my chair, sprint down the aisle, rush past the professor who walks in as I'm running off, and, uh...

"Mr. Jackson! Class is about to start!" he shouts. "Where are you going?"

"Sorry, emergency!" I yell back, halfway down the hall hoping he hears me.

CHARLOTTE

I have a free period so I'm, um... sitting in the art club room, doodling some Valentine's Day ideas. It doesn't really

21

make sense for my story, but I'm sketching a cute heart-themed candlelit dinner between Huntley and Chantel.

In my sketch, they're sitting at a table in a cozy Italian restaurant and Huntley tried to dress up but it's just, um... a tucked in flannel shirt and khaki pants. In contrast, Chantel's wearing a flowy red dress that's tighter up top and shaped like a heart around her bust. Her boobs and the dress look heart-shaped and Huntley's staring while pretending to look at the menu and, um...

So that's what I'm doing and it's going well except then Hunter storms into the room, slams the door behind him, and just kind of stands there, huffing and puffing.

I jump, startled, and nearly fling my notebook at him because, um... I mistake him for someone dangerous at first. I wield my sketchpad like a throwing knife and Hunter lifts one brow, staring at me.

"Dude," he says, frantic.

"Dude," I say, confused.

"Can you try not to murder me with your sketchpad?" he asks. "Thanks."

"D-don't scare me then!" I snap.

"What're you drawing?"

I show him the sketch and he nods and looks at all the little bits and bobs I added in for, um... I just put a lot of fun random details and I'm really enjoying my drawing time so far.

"Cool. It's great," he says. "Seriously."

"Um, you don't sound serious at all, though?" I point out.

"No, I am. But... I fucked up."

"...Did you eat too much chocolate?"

"No? Huh? Why would you ask that?" he says, cocking his head to the side.

"It was the first thing I thought of," I whine. "Like, um... maybe you have a tummy ache and that's why you screwed up?"

"Can you say that again?"

"...What part?"

"The tummy ache part? Cute as fuck."

"Don't tease me!" I mumble. "Maybe you d-do have a tummy ache after all..."

"I'll give you a tummy ache..." he says, which, um... the way he says it is growly and flirty but I don't even know how this is a flirty thing to say?

"Please don't," I murmur back. "I think that'd be like cramps and I really don't want cramps today."

"I was going more with, you know, we'll make love and I'll be so far inside you your tummy would, uh... let's go with a good ache? It was a shitty pickup line. Sorry."

"...Yes that's really bad..." I say, trying to let him down easy. "Also, um... we... we'll... m-make love?"

Hunter stares at me and I stare back and I kind of wonder if that's what the emergency is and are we going to do it now because there's a perfectly good table right in front of me and I don't know if we should make love in the art club room on one of the drawing tables but for Valentine's Day it suddenly seems like a perfectly great idea, so...

"I don't have rose petals," Hunter grunts, gritting his teeth. "That's what I came to tell you. Seriously, fuck. I can't even believe this."

"Oh," I say, patting him lightly on the shoulder because he looks pretty upset about this. "It's okay? We can get some?"

"Dude, that's the thing!" he counters despairingly. "Look, I wanted to get you flowers and I wanted something you'd like so I went with the tulips because they looked good and I picked them out on my own and... I literally couldn't get roses even if I wanted to. I went to the goddamn grocery store this morning and even they were cleaned out of the things. I walked to every corner store I could find and... nothing. There aren't any roses, Baby Sis. The roses are gone. Valentine's Day is ruined."

"I don't think it's *ruined*," I say, because, um... I mean we still have each other. That's the important part, right? "But, um... tomorrow?"

"Tomorrow's tomorrow," Hunter philosophizes. "Today's today, Baby Sis."

"That, um... that's usually how days work?"

"Dude, come on," he says, sighing.

"What!"

"No, for real, are there any loopholes? Can I completely blow your mind without rose petals somehow?"

"You can... tomorrow?" I repeat, just in case he forgot that part.

"I meant today. I need a loophole today."

"Um, there aren't any, though? Angela made us all agree and..."

"What if I text her?" Hunter asks, desperate.

"You're going to text Angela and ask how we can make love on Valentine's Day without rose petals?" I ask, repeating his thought process back to him in case he doesn't realize what he's asking. "Um, strange but okay?"

"When you say it like that..." Hunter groans. "Fuck."

"What if, um... I... I have an idea!"

"I'm in," he says instantly. "Let's do it."

I mean, he just said we can do it so I guess I don't have to explain?

Right, so...

HUNTER

Baby Sis drags me to...

It's an arts and crafts shop. I've never been in an arts and crafts shop and I don't even know what they have, but holy fucking shit they have *everything*.

How many arts and crafts are there? All of them,

apparently. All the fucking arts and crafts you could ever dream of.

We pass a candlemaking section, which I never realized was a thing until now. There's a massive wall of literally every color of construction paper you can imagine. Then there's sewing, knitting, crochet, and all that old lady grandma stuff. And, uh... we don't stop at any of that and instead make a beeline for a section marked as Decorative Flowers. Is this an art or a craft? I don't know and I don't understand at first, but then--

Holy fucking shit, it's *perfect!*

Nobody said we needed *real* roses, right? If we get fake roses with, you know, fake petals? Game on, motherfuckers! Screw you Angela and your weird ass rumor bullshit! I win!

I don't say that out loud, but come on, why is Angela trying to cockblock everyone on Valentine's Day?

Suddenly everything's looking up except then Baby Sis and I stand in front of the shelves of decorative flowers and--

"Ummm..." she mumbles, staring at the same empty section for roses that I am.

"Fuck," I grunt.

An employee wanders over, sees us staring at the empty decorative roses section, and offers us a consolatory nod.

"Sorry," she says. "We're getting more in soon. We usually sell a few for Valentine's Day but most people prefer the real thing. Tons of people came in this year asking if we sold roses, though. Rose petals? They're made of cloth so you can pull the petals off. We're even sold out of bags full of rose petals. It's actually pretty cute! I'm glad everyone's getting into the mood and trying new crafts."

"Soon," I say, narrowing in on that one word. "But... not today?"

"Next week."

"Um, s-sorry!" Baby Sis stammers. "I tried?"

"It's not your fault," I say. "Don't even worry about it."

"Can we still spend Valentine's Day together?" she asks, as if I'm on the verge of canceling it or something.

"Yeah, no, uh... I mean, yeah, of course," I say, trying to hide my disappointment. "It's fine. Maybe it's better this way? We can be totally romantic and, like... cuddle up while watching a movie and fall asleep and..."

I mean, look, that's obviously *fine,* but... dude, today's *Valentine's Day.*

If I can't make love to my girlfriend on Valentine's Day, what's even the point?

...Besides the cuddling, kissing, and falling asleep together part...

Anyways, I don't want her seeing me pout like a baby so...

"You need to get to class soon, right?" I say. "I'm gonna hang out here for a second and look around. For, uh... no reason."

"If you need time alone to be sad, I understand," she says, sneaking in a hug.

"Yeah, kinda," I admit. "Thanks, Baby Sis."

She squeezes me tight one last time and leaves me to it. The woman working there looks like she's about to laugh, because I'm probably being way too dramatic, and, uh...

Wait. Fuck. I have an idea. It's amazing. Why didn't I think of it earlier?

Nobody said we need *real* rose petals!

I'm a goddamn genius.

CHARLOTTE

Hunter and I are having a quiet Valentine's Day because we have class the next day and, um... we have class on Valentine's Day too, so...

We get pizza to go at our favorite pizza place and we even get loaded waffle fries with extra fried jalapenos and we head back to the dorms to watch a movie that definitely won't be a horror movie because I told him we needed to watch a romantic movie for Valentine's Day, and...

He seems like he's in a better mood? He's smiling and teasing me again and he looks excited for pizza and now *I'm* excited for pizza and... we can still cuddle and kiss, right?

I remember texting Angela after I left Hunter earlier, because I felt bad and I was just kind of hopeful, you know?

> "I know you said we need rose petals if we're going to have a booty call but what if it's hand and mouth stuff? Do we need rose petals for that?"

Her answer?

ANGELA

> "Babe, Charlie, I get it, and I hope you and Hunter have a great one, but, no. Solidarity, babe, remember? You can totally give him the blowjob of his dreams but you need to make sure he has rose petals on the bed or else what's the point? Same with hand stuff. Clarissa asked if she could send her stepbrother a video of her playing with herself because they haven't seen each other for awhile and, like, even THAT needs rose petals, which she agreed to and said it sounded even more fun, so... you understand, right?"

So, um... I'm sorry, Hunter... I tried so hard...

Maybe that's why he's excited but if so I'm going to have to let him down and then--

I'm trying to think of how to tell him as we walk into his dorm room with our food and my laptop so we can watch a movie when suddenly the telltale scent of roses overwhelms me. It's a lot of rose scent. Like, um... I don't want to say *too* much because I like it, but it's more than I expected considering neither of us could find roses, real, fake, or otherwise?

Scattered across his bed in all their rosy, floral-scented wonder, are--

At first it looks like actual rose petals and I stare at his bed, slightly awed, mostly excited. Because, um, I can give him a blowjob now? Or we can make love! Or both? That sounds fun. If Hunter wants to do something to me too, that's great. I'm all for it, really.

It's not real rose petals, though. It's red construction paper, intricately and intimately cut into rose petal shapes. There's red construction paper hearts scattered in, too. Most are red, but he snuck in a few pink ones, as well. It's literally the entire bed, fully covered with red and pink construction paper cutouts of rose petals and hearts that really smell like roses.

"I got the idea at the arts and crafts place," Hunter says, grinning. "We passed the construction paper and there was that candlemaking section, remember? I bought a hundred sheets of paper and rose-scented oil for making candles, and... ta da!"

"I love it," I say, staring at the bed, way too excited. "It's so pretty, too."

Hunter smirks. He puts the pizza box and waffle fries on his desk and slides close, holding me tight.

"Happy Valentine's Day, Baby Sis," he says, kissing me softly.

"Happy Valentine's Day," I say, kissing him back.

Our lips linger and, um... our pizza's probably getting cold but that's fine because kissing's more important to me right now. I keep glancing at the bed every few seconds, winking my eyes open as we kiss. Hunter sees me and rolls his eyes, laughing.

"We're going to eat this, alright?" he says, nodding towards the food.

"Alright," I say, nodding back.

"Later," he adds, digging his fingers into my hips.

"Late--" I start to say, except then, um...

Hunter picks me up and tosses me onto his bed, a spray of paper petals scattering everywhere. I squeal and laugh and kick my feet, which somehow makes it easier for him to take my shoes off? I don't even know how, but he does it. And then, you know...

I help. We strip as quickly as possible, rose petals flying, until we're completely naked and Hunter has a bunch of paper petals stuck to his chest. I reach up and pluck one off, giggling at it while he smirks at me, slipping between my thighs.

Oh gosh.

I... I wasn't expecting this so quickly or suddenly, but before I know it he has the head of his, um... it's lodged between my lower lips and then it's not even lodged, it's inside me, and my eyes roll into the back of my head while I fumble with the rose petal in my fingers. He thrusts all the way inside me, feeling my wetness. It's easy with him. I feel like we could just do it, any time or place, whenever, and it'd always be easy with him...

I don't know if this is making love yet but I want it to be.

Hunter pushes in and slides his hands up my body. He grins at the fact that I now have a rose-scented heart covering one nipple. He flicks it aside while I watch, squirming and wriggling beneath him. He replaces the heart with his mouth and sucks my nipple between his lips.

I gasp, bucking my hips, pressing against his core. He lets me, teasing me with his mouth. He reaches up with his other hand and caresses my cheek and, um... I don't really think about it and it kind of happens on accident but his thumb gets close to my lips and it's right there, so...

I trace the tip of my tongue against his teasing thumb and when he drags it closer I wrap my lips around it and suck lightly. In response, I feel him throb and pulse inside me, excited. I twist and twirl my tongue around his thumb as if it's something else entirely and I'm rewarded with more throbbing, pulsing goodness.

"I just wanted to feel you," he says after one last lick, circling the outer edge of my nipple. "I wasn't planning on finishing this so soon."

"C-can we, um... make love, though?" I ask, trailing my tongue across the pad of his thumb.

Hunter groans, eyes rolling into the back of his head. I like that he likes that. It's fun and different and new and...

He opens his eyes, gazing into mine. "Yeah. We have before, you know?"

"...Have we?"

I, um... I don't want to ask too much but... if we've *made* love before, does that mean...

I blush and squirm and I don't even know how to ask that or what to say or... *oh gosh...*

Hunter kisses me hard, shifting like he's about to pull out, except at the last second he thrusts back in. I gasp, my mouth opening over his kiss. While I'm trying to regain some small amount of composure, he actually pulls out next time and--

My composure is gone in about a second as he changes from kissing my regular lips to, um... you know, kissing the lower ones. It's not even kissing so much as greedily sliding his tongue between them and coaxing my ecstatic pearl with the tip of his tongue. He holds my thighs, spread, while he laps up my wetness, savoring me, teasing me, tormenting me. I arch my back and gasp and moan and...

I don't want to say Angela's rose petal booty call idea is *bad,* because I like the *idea* of it, but in practice it's a lot different?

As I thrust my hips up, instinctively pushing against

Hunter's mouth, a spray of paper petals flutters around our naked bodies. It's kind of a lot. I know rose petals was the point, but seeing them on the bed is different from having them flying and fluttering around us as we enjoy each other's bodies. I'm not even enjoying Hunter's body yet and it's still happening. He's just enjoying mine. I feel kind of left out?

I blink my eyes open and watch him through a cloud of construction paper cutouts. It's like a romance movie in real life, except he has paper stuck in his hair and across his back. I don't even want to know where they'll end up afterwards.

Is this like glitter? We'll find petals everywhere for the next two weeks?

Also, um... I can see his hardness... and...

Hunter's lower half is propped up, hovering above the bed as he torments me with his tongue. He's so close and yet so far. I can see, but I can't touch. Trust me, I'm trying. I reach and stretch and, um... my arms aren't long enough. It's very sad.

Hunter realizes I'm doing something different and he pulls his tongue away from his current Valentine's Day activity.

"You okay?" he asks.

"Yes, but--"

I, um... I tell him what my frustration's are and... um...

"H-Hunter!" I gasp as he flips the script. I didn't even realize there was a script before but we had one and it's been flipped.

Suddenly instead of me laying on the bed, he is. And I'm laying on him. Except his head's between my thighs and my head's--

He's right there, ready for the taking, staring at me with eager excitement. His manhood throbs and bounces just below my lips. This is, um... it's a new position and we've never done this before and honestly I'm pretty excited.

My excitement is interrupted by him burying his tongue against my clit. Oh gosh, this is going to be hard, isn't it?

I gasp and squirm but apparently in his new vantage point, he can more easily hold me down? He wraps his arms around my legs, hands gripping my butt, basically pulling me against his mouth as he tries to distract me from what I eagerly want.

Frantic, trying to control myself for a fraction of a second so I can at least *try*, I, um... I wrap my fingers around his shaft, gasping and panting and already beyond excited. I open my mouth wide and bob my head lower and take the head of his shaft between my lips.

Hunter lets out a lusty groan as I take him. He forgets himself for a second, slowing down on tormenting me to further ecstasy. Basically I have just enough time to stroke him up and down twice before he redoubles his efforts.

Maybe even tripled at this point.

I have him in my sights, though. Locked on and targeted. Don't even try it, Hunter!

...Please keep trying it I really like this...

As he tries to make me orgasm first, I do the same. He focuses on my clit, knowing what I like. I slide my tongue across his head and stroke him faster and faster, pushing him closer to the edge. We're on even ground, I think. I don't really know because every time he moans it's directly against my lower lips and, um... I'm pretty sure I'm moaning a lot too but my mouth is full, so...

Oh gosh, it's happening.

I gasp and try my best to keep him in my mouth but my O is coming on hard and he's so focused and intent and it just smells really nice and this is Valentine's Day and, um...

He finishes a second after me. I pull him into my mouth, tasting him, but then he, um... he pops free and now it's spraying everywhere and oh gosh, it's a lot.

We finish like that, somehow, and I lay in a heap on him,

upside-down. Hunter does the same except he's upside-down to me but maybe he's technically rightside-up since his head's on the pillows?

Anyways--

I squirm and roll over and cuddle close to him, ignoring our mess. It's not just the sticky mess, it's the millions of paper petals everywhere.

"Holy fuck," Hunter says, wide-eyed. "What was that?"

"Um, a lot of fun?" I say, giggling.

He laughs. "Not what I meant, but yeah, it was."

"...Are we still going to make love?"

"Uh huh..."

"Pizza first?"

"Definitely."

"Yay!"

We eat pizza and watch a silly romance movie on Netflix. We... don't bother putting our clothes back on? And... halfway through the movie...

"H-Hunter!" I gasp as he fits inside me perfectly. It's like we were made for this. I know he's the only one I've ever been with but I don't care. I did it right on the first try, I guess? That's a silly romance novel idea I read once but seriously, it's the perfect size and I feel so full and satisfied and...

We finish together this time, at the same time, slow and sweet, soft and nice. I squeeze him tight and he presses hard inside me and I can feel him filling me in more ways than one. I don't even think about the mess this time. After my shower plan, um... I think it's fine if we do this wherever? We can always clean up later, right?

Hunter rains kisses across my cheeks and my face and my lips until I start to giggle and squirm. He's still inside me, which, um... I think I make him excited again because he starts throbbing and comes back to life.

"Was that making love?" I ask, looking into his eyes and seeing beautiful dark stars.

"It was," he says, smiling and kissing me softly, hugging me tight.

"Thanks," I say, trying not to giggle.

Hunter snickers. "Anytime."

"Um, do you want to go to McReynold's for breakfast tomorrow?" I ask before I forget. "We, um... I mean, me and Angela and Clarissa and Jenny are going and... hashbrowns and breakfast sandwiches?"

"Are you trying to make me make love to you again? Because that's a good way to make me make love to you again."

"Um, if you want to, but that wasn't why I--!"

I try to say more but Hunter's ready and willing to keep his promise, so...

Happy Valentine's Day to me?

AMATEUR NIGHT

Episode 164

CHARLOTTE

CHLOE

"ROOMIE! Everything's all set. I've got the goods. Tell everyone to meet in that creepy dark alley between the cafeteria and the gym and I'll hand IDs out there. What time's your big show, by the way? Can't wait! Seriously, you're amazing."

That's, um... that's Chloe and apparently the fake IDs for my romance book club friends and Amelia are all set. Oh, and Jenny. I didn't ask, but Angela and Clarissa are good to go, too. They have their own already.

Which leaves me with one final important task before heading to the stripclub to compete against, um... I mean, it's mainly supposed to be Erica but I don't think everyone would appreciate it if we tried to commandeer the entire competition for selfish purposes? No one at the stripclub even knows us.

I do know one of the strippers already, Bella, but I'm not sure that counts.

Also Jenny, Clarissa, and Angela wanted to join amateur

night too and I don't want to ruin it for them. Plus I think it'll be fun to dance with my friends even if I'm not technically dancing *with* them, you know? They'll do their dance, I'll do mine, and we can cheer and support each other from the sidelines!

...I don't think there's sidelines in a stripclub but I don't actually know *what* there is so, um...

Anyways, I text Hunter because I need him.

> "Hi, I need you. I know it's supposed to be my own thing, but can you go to the stripclub with me? I want to get there early so I know what to do. I'm really nervous. I think if I get there earlier it'll be easier for me? I don't know why I'm asking you to come because I don't know what you're supposed to do there. I guess you can't come in the dressing room with me, huh? Actually, nevermind. I can go alone. It's fine. I'm fine. I'll be fine. Okay bye see you later, please don't forget about me, I need you."

Admittedly I probably shouldn't have sent that but it took me awhile to write everything and by the end I figured there was no point in *not* sending it, so... I did.

And, um, yes, right, so...

Hunter replies?

HUNTER

"Dude, of course I'll come early. It's cool. I don't know anything about stripper dressing rooms, though. Not sure how that works. I can hang in the club while you get dressed? I promise I won't toss a wad of cash at any other girls no matter how hard they shake their booty at me. Saving my dollar bills for you, Baby Sis. Aw yeah. That was supposed to be sweet but right after I typed it I realized it's kind of a dick thing to say. I was just joking, though."

"It's okay. I know. If a girl is really good at shaking her butt I think you can give her a dollar and tell her it's from me?"

"I think most strippers would get offended if I only gave them a dollar so I'll pass but thanks for looking out."

"Oh. Right. I didn't think about that. You can give me a dollar if I'm really good at shaking my butt, though? I won't get offended."

"I already know you're good at shaking that booty, Baby Sis. Gonna fucking throw every dollar I have on stage when you're dancing. Hell yeah. Goddamn, I'm so excited for this. Do I get a private dance later or what? How much is that?"

"I'm not actually going to take your money! I'll give it back later, alright? If you want a private dance you have to be super nice to me and you have to be honest about if you like my dance or not and also maybe call me a good girl and say how proud of me you are and if it's not too late after can we get something to eat because I think I'll be hungry?"

"Sure. To all of that. Sounds good. When are we heading over?"

"Is now good?"

"Fuck. Yeah, I guess? Hold up. Let me finish getting ready. I'll meet you out front in fifteen minutes. Sound good?"

"Yes please thank you see you soon!"

And so...

"So... no offense, but I'm not sure this is the kind of outfit you wear when you're planning on dancing at a stripclub?" Hunter says, looking me up and down.

"What, why?" I ask, pretending like I'm planning on doing that.

I'm not, but, um... I don't want to tell him what I'm wearing yet. It's a secret, Hunter! Shhh...

"I guess it's what's underneath that's important?" he offers with a shrug. "Wait, are you stripping or not? I got confused. You don't have to."

"...Shhhhhh," I murmur, pressing a finger against his lips. "It's a secret..."

"You're wearing some stupidly hot lingerie, aren't you?" he asks, acting as if he has X-ray vision and can see under my jeans and pale blue tee. "Is it the sexy black negligee? Because, yeah, it's hot, but I don't know if that's proper stripper attire either..."

"I'm not telling you!" I say, standing up for myself, hands on my hips and everything.

I wiggle them side to side, trying to do a sort of standing

in place sashay like Angela or Clarissa would, but I think it's just a wiggle. I do my best, though.

"Fuck, you're so hot when you get feisty with me..." Hunter growls. "This is kind of weird though, huh? I mean, I'm totally down to see you dance on a pole, but everyone else is going to see you dance on a pole too, so, uh..."

"Nope, I'm only going to dance for you," I say, simple and sweet. "B-but can we, um... can we leave soon because..."

Hunter smirks and sneaks in for a quick kiss. "Already on it."

He sweeps me into his arms under the guise of, um... you know, sweeping me off my feet? Which he does, except after the kissing and sweeping he also opens the back door of a car that just pulled up and continues sweeping me inside of it. I land butt first in the back and scoot over fast so Hunter can slide in while our Uber driver blinks and stares at us like we're crazy.

"Hey," he says, nodding from the front. "Hunter?"

"Yeah," Hunter says.

"And you're going to..." the driver says, reading the end location off his phone.

"Yeah," Hunter says as the guy trails off, possibly embarrassed.

"Uh, okay, sure."

And... we're off!

Before we arrive at the club, I text the girl power group chat and let them know what's going on. Chloe's in it now and she's really excited about that.

It's just a short text saying I went ahead early and they don't have to come early but if they *want* to come early then they *can* come early and, um... yes.

That's it.

Quick, I put my phone away because I'm kind of anxious now even if Hunter's with me and, um... what do I do when I get there?

...I didn't think this all the way through...

The driver pulls up outside the club. It's a relatively big building close to the off ramp of the highway, a large parking lot circling it on most sides. The lights in the stripclub's parking lot glare down on every possible shadow to ever exist within a hundred yard radius, as if there can be no possible shady dealings whatsoever happening here. Also I think that makes it safer? I mean, if I were a stripper and I had to walk around out here I'd really appreciate the light a lot. It just seems safer.

...Wait, I'm technically a stripper tonight?

Do I feel safer...?

Um, yes, kind of?

...Mostly because I'm with Hunter but I think the lights help a little...

"You sure this is the right spot?" the driver asks, slowly idling the car to a stop near the front.

"Um, yes?" I say. "W-wait! Are there other stripclubs, um... around... around here?"

"Dude," Hunter says, rolling his eyes.

"What! I don't know. Maybe this isn't the right one?"

"I mean, there's a few about a hundred miles south of here," the driver says, shrugging.

"See?" Hunter says to me. "This is it. This is the right place. I mean, you can text Erica if you want but please don't. Fuck, she really pisses me off. Like, holy shit, I'm excited about this but then I keep remembering it's because of her and I get really pissed off. Please kick her ass, alright?"

"I don't think that's allowed?" I say. "We're only supposed to dance."

"...Dude."

"No offense but I have another person to pick up, so if you

two could, you know... get out?" the driver asks as politely as possible.

Which we then do, hopping out fast. I scurry after Hunter and cling to his arm while we walk to the entrance of the club. A pretty neon sign above the door says **"PAPER SLIPPER"** with a neat neon-stylized outline of a ballet slipper right next to it. Or maybe it's like Cinderella's glass slipper? Except this one is paper for unknown reasons.

A very large man in a suit confronts us at the entrance, blocking our way before we can even get inside.

"ID," he says, staring at us from behind dark sunglasses.

It's both intimidating but also kind of confusing because it's dusk and even though there's a small amount of sunlight left it's nowhere near enough to need sunglasses. The parking lot lights *are* really bright, though?

"Um... hi," I say, nervously reaching into my pocket for my fake ID. I accidentally pull out my phone instead and start to hand it to him but then realize the error of my ways halfway there. I anxiously put my phone back in my pocket and take out my fake ID instead, but by then Hunter already has his.

"Lady's first?" Hunter says, smiling and reassuring me.

"Um, no, you can go first..." I mumble.

The bouncer looks amused and annoyed at our interaction. He swipes both mine and Hunter's IDs from our hands and glares at them. Just in case, because, I don't know why, he lifts his sunglasses to inspect them better.

"These fakes?" he asks.

Oh gosh he knows and now I have to tell the truth because I can't lie and I think that means I lose this part of the Stepbrother Triathlon by default but it's not like I can help it. I'm sorry, Hunter! I wanted to fight for you so much!

"No," Hunter says, lying.

The bouncer grins. "Just checking. Wait, are you her? I thought she said your name was Charlotte?"

Shoot.

"That's... m-my middle name?" I mumble. "Ummm... wait, who... who said that?"

"Bella. She said to look out for some timid mousy girl. You might be with friends or a guy, she wasn't sure. You the guy?" he asks, turning to Hunter.

"I guess so?" Hunter says, as confused as I am.

"Cool. Name's Bruno. I'll keep an eye out for you two. Alright? You can't head into the girls' room even if you're with her, though. She's got to go in alone."

"Do, um... do I have to stay in there, though?" I ask.

"It's a dressing room, not a prison," Bruno says, and I think he's rolling his eyes at me from behind his sunglasses but I can't tell for sure. "Go in whenever you want and come out whenever you want. It's just amateur night. Usually quiet, but some of the guys get off on seeing new girls. Don't let anyone fuck with you, though. If you feel unsafe or someone's doing shit you don't like, tell me and I'll deal with it. Got it?"

"Did you hear that?" I say to Hunter. "That means you have to be nice to me tonight."

"I was going to be nice to you anyways," Hunter says, smirking.

"Yeah, better be nice to your girl, buddy," Bruno says, taking my side. "You're big but I'm bigger."

Hunter gives him a fake salute. "Yes, sir."

"Don't do that," Bruno says, glaring at him. "Bella's waiting, by the way. Says she has everything ready. Don't let the girls fuck with you, either. I can't do much about them. Just stick up for yourself if they try to start shit. It's better that way."

"...Um, okay..." I mumble, because... oh gosh, I didn't even think about that...

I hope they like me?

HUNTER

I didn't have a plan when tonight started. I have no idea what the fuck I'm doing. This is my stepsister's big night and she's here to show my evil ex-girlfriend once and for all that, no, fuck you, Erica, your weird ass stepbro fetish is dumb so leave us the hell alone forever, thanks.

Right. This is that night, and since Baby Sis already won the last impromptu event and it's the best two-out-of-three for the triathlon, well...

Once she wins the amateur night competition, that's it. Bye, Erica!

That's how I'm hoping it'll go but I don't expect Erica to play fair and I'm sure she has something up her sleeve...

So instead of watching a couple of girls rhythmically dance on poles by themselves because there's barely anyone here right now since it's way too early, uh... I text Sam and Olly and Teddy.

I even made us a group text chat which feels really fucked up but seriously my alternatives are... staring at this Latina girl who is *really* good at pole dancing, or watching a stupidly busty blonde who is somehow doing a handstand *and* shaking her boobs in this one dude's face at the same time, or, uh... you know, texting my bros, so...

"Guys, what the fuck, where are you?"

Olly replies first:

OLLY

"Jacksy, did you add us to a group chat?"

Sam's next:

SAM

"This is it, boys! Hell yeah. I've been waiting for a group chat forever. I know we don't text often, but how useful is this?"

43

And finally Teddy:

TEDDY

"Do I need a special ringtone for the group chat, too? I'll think of a good one. Oh, hey, where are you guys, though? Jenny said to meet her in between the cafeteria and the gym? I don't get it."

I wish I could explain this to them but I don't know how, so...

"I'm at the stripclub already. Baby Sis wanted to get here early. She's in the dressing room with some chick named Bella. I guess she knows her from somewhere? Anyways, hurry your asses up. I don't want to sit here by myself."

Olly has opinions:

OLLY

"Dude, you're in a stripclub. If you're alone, you're doing it wrong. Go chat up a stripper or something?"

Teddy is kind of useless. Sorry, Teddy.

TEDDY

"Guys, there's like six other girls here? Oh, wait, Angela and Clarissa are here, too. I don't think nine of us can fit in one Uber, can we?"

Sam's the only helpful one. Thanks, Sam.

SAM

"Amelia and I are coming. We're sharing an Uber with Chloe. Have the book club girls ride together, and then you, Jenny, Angela, and Clarissa can go together, too."

Olly has *more* opinions...

OLLY

"What about me, asshole?"

Sam is somehow even *more* helpful. Goddamn, dude. Putting in work.

SAM

"Amelia told Hannah we're all sharing rides to the club, Olly. Meaning, if you're not a complete dick to me, I'll get you in the same car as her. What do you say, buddy?"

OLLY

"Yes. If I say more I'll fuck this up so let's stick with that."

SAM

"Good idea, man. Meet her in the library parking lot. Say Sam and Amelia sent you. Gotta book the ride yourself, though. Figure it out."

OLLY

"Dude, I know how to order an Uber. I'm not an idiot. Thanks, though. Seriously. Wait, fuck, did you say anything else to her?!"

SAM

"Nah, you're good. Shoot your shot, player."

It's at that point I decide to rejoin the chat against my better judgement.

> "I seriously regret making this group chat now. Can I delete it?"

I'm outvoted with three immediate *No's,* so I guess that's the answer. Fuck you guys.

Also I'm suddenly approached by a stripper and I have to figure out how to tell her to go away in the nicest and least offensive way possible, so...

CHARLOTTE

I have time before the competition starts, at least according to a sign on the wall that says:

THURSDAYS
$1000 AMATEUR NIGHT
AMATEUR NIGHT EVERY THURSDAY

LADIES SIGN UP BY 9PM
MUST BE 18+ TO ENTER *(CONTEST ONLY)*
[Now Hiring Dancers]

...Apparently I didn't need a fake ID for amateur night...

Um, the other girls did, though. Chloe and my friends from the romance book club. I feel bad about lying to Bruno now and I kind of want to go back and apologize and show him my real ID and tell him, um... I was nervous b-but I'm eighteen and I'm only here for amateur night so, um...

S-sorry, Bruno!

Except before I can do that Bella spies me standing awkwardly on the really plush red carpets in the stripclub with Hunter and steals me away.

"Charlotte and I have business to attend to," she says to Hunter. "You're cute, though. Gia will love you. Meaning, stay away from her until Charlotte's back. She'll try her best, though. Just warning you."

Bella winks at Hunter after that and I don't know if she's kidding or not but when I look at the girl Bella indicates is Gia, um... wow, she's really pretty.

She's the darker skinned Latina slowly dancing her way around the pole at the opposite side of the main showroom. At first I think she's naked but she's actually wearing a leather bra and panties that are almost the same color as her skin. Just in case that was too much color matching, she's wearing sky-high sky blue heels. They contrast really well with her honey brown hair. I understand why the man sitting by her pole is enthusiastically placing dollar bills in a pile for her. He's very polite about it, too.

And then I'm stolen into the back before I even have time to say goodbye to Hunter.

I say it anyways just in case he can still hear me.

"B-bye!" I squeak, getting dragged down a dark hallway to who knows where.

"Seriously, you're too cute," Bella says, laughing. "It's nice, though. Refreshing. I wish I could be that cute about a boy. But, well... been burned too many times and I have a kid to take care of, so..."

"Um, what does your daughter do when you're working?" I ask.

...I belatedly realize I don't know if I'm supposed to ask questions like that or not?

"My sister watches her," Bella says, calm, friendly. "I don't mind, but no one asks about that here. It's one of those things, you know?"

"Um, no..." I mumble, because I've never been a stripper before.

Bella laughs. "Good. Look, this is fun and it's not fun. Tonight'll be fun, but the more you do this, the less fun it gets and the more you realize it's a job and actual hard work. I'm not saying that to scare you. I just want you to know that tonight you'll feel like Cinderella heading to the ball, but don't get used to it, alright?"

"I... I won't," I say, nodding seriously. "I promise."

"Good. Now let's see how you look with some over the top makeup and your new outfit, shall we?"

"Oh. Okay? Um, I didn't know I had to do my makeup, though? I didn't bring any?"

"Charlotte," Bella says, shaking her head. "You don't even have the kind of makeup I'm talking about. Don't worry. I've got you covered. You just need to sit down and let me do my thing then tell me what you think. Understood?"

I nod, taking this seriously, hoping I'm not, um... too far in over my head? Because I really feel like I am right now but I don't know yet.

Also the dark hallway is getting less dark by the second and we're headed towards a door with light shining through the bottom. A bunch of loud, boisterous women are animatedly talking from behind the door, which Bella suddenly shoves open, pushing me inside.

She stands back, letting me take it all in.

It's, um...

I don't even know.

Wow...

"Ladies," Bella says, vaguely acknowledging the woman standing, sitting, and strutting around the dressing room. "This is Charlotte. I'm taking care of her tonight. She won't be here long, so don't pull any of that new girl bullshit with her. She's here for amateur night. That's it."

"If that's it, why are you bringing her here?" a woman wearing a barely-there micro bikini asks. "You don't *do* favors, Bella."

Bella rolls her eyes. "Go to hell, Crystal. I do what I want. Everyone knows that. And I want to do this. Charlotte's cool."

"She looks nervous," Crystal says, grinning. "You nervous, new girl?"

"Um, yes," I say, nodding very fast.

"You're not supposed to admit it," Bella says, laughing. "But coming from you, it works. Happy, Crystal?"

"No, not really. I wanted to see her get her hackles up. It's more fun."

"S-sorry!" I squeak. "Um... n-no... I'm not nervous at all...?"

"Love her already. This'll be fun. Can she even dance? What's her deal? She's clearly not here to strip."

"Don't worry about it," Bella says, shrugging off the question. "Charlotte, come. Ignore the mess. It'd be worse but there's less girls working tonight. I'll show you around then we'll work on your look, alright?"

"...Okay..." I say, and I'm now positive I'm in way over my head but this is my night and I need to fight for Hunter!

...I don't actually need to fight for Hunter but if I can't fight for Hunter then what kind of girlfriend am I...

"So," Bella says, strutting through the changing room with practiced efficiency. "There's a few new girls tonight. You can tell by how excited they look to be here. Which means Crystal clearly isn't new and she's been here forever, so she's a major bitch."

Crystal cackles, witchy. "Thanks, Bella!"

Bella ignores her and points out a group of younger women chatting excitedly amongst themselves in one corner of the room. "That spot's for newbies. They either stay for a few weeks before realizing it's not as glamorous as they expected, or they make it to the middle of the room once they commit. It's an unspoken rule. No one knows how it started, it just keeps going like that. It's also a major source of drama and some girls take bets on who is going to backstab who. It's not very classy. I hate it."

"Um, what if none of them backstabs anyone and they're all really nice?" I ask.

"Cute," Bella says, snickering. "Never gonna happen, but that's cute."

She struts past racks of, um... they're clothes but also I don't know if anyone would ever call these clothes? They're pieces of fabric that can be worn in some semblance of body coverage, but, um... barely? Strips of cloth that probably wrap around somewhere and hide something but I don't know what, itty bitty bikini tops or bottoms, a few pairs of what I assume are shorts but the tiniest pairs I've ever seen. There's a couple of feather boas for good measure and those look nice but also I don't know how you'd pole dance with one because it seems like it'd fall off or get stuck.

"So, introductions," Bella says, nodding to the longterm girls once we get to the other side. "You don't have to say hi. Anyone worth talking to will say hi to you instead. It's better if you don't--"

"Um, h-hello..." I say, awkwardly waving to the room.

I thought this was when I was supposed to say hi and I was anxiously waiting for Bella to mention it. My brain didn't really catch up with the exact words she was saying so, um... when she said the introductions part... I started waving and it took me a second to realize I *shouldn't* be waving, so...

"Charlotte," Bella says, flat.

"I didn't mean to do that," I whisper, apologetic.

"The new girl's *amazing!*" Crystal yells. "Hey, new girl!"

I wave back. "Hi."

I know she's teasing me but I want to be nice.

"Charlotte..." Bella says, flatter.

"I'm sorry I'm very bad at this."

"You are. It's fine," she says with a jaded sigh. "Anyways, for unknown reasons, strippers generally come in a few easy to categorize flavors."

I have no idea what that means and I don't know if I'm supposed to taste a certain way so I just listen.

"Stripper names," Bella clarifies. "Everyone needs one. You have the Gemstones. Those are girls named after gems, like Crystal, Ruby, Jade, and Amber over there. Then Animals, which includes names like Kitty, Bunny, Fawn, and Bambi. There's the Sweets: Cinnamon, Candy, Cherry, Coco. And last but not least, you have what I like to call the Charms, or girls who pick names and play up the primal meaning behind them. I'm talking Chastity, Serenity, Lola, and Angel."

"My mom's name is Bunny," I say, because it seems topical. "Ummm... it's short for Barbara, though?"

Bella stares at me as if I'm a complex math problem she knows how to solve but doesn't want to.

"You forgot the Exotics!" a Gemstone girl shouts, somehow strutting over to us wearing the tallest high heels I've ever seen. She doesn't stumble or anything. "Hey. I'm Ruby. I've heard so much about you!"

"Um, you have?"

Bella shrugs; apparently it wasn't her.

"From Angela and Clarissa. Aw, I'm so proud of them! My girls! So cute, right? You're here together, right?"

"They, um... they aren't here yet... b-but yes?"

"Great!"

"What are Exotics?" I ask, curious.

"It's a dumb term Ruby made up for strippers with names that don't fall into another category," Bella says, immediately sounding grumpy about it.

Ruby winks at me. "Bella's mad because she's an Exotic."

"I wasn't *anything* until you came up with that stupid name."

"Anyways!" Ruby says, giggly. She totally reminds me of the cheerleaders. "Exotics have exotic names. Like Bella, Gia, Yasmin, and so on."

"There's the Girls Next Door, too," Bella adds. "They're

boring. Lexi, Lacy, Jenna."

"I think I understand?" I say.

"Do you?" Bella asks, turning on me, grinning wider, almost wicked.

"What Bella means is it's your turn," Ruby says, excited. "If you could be anyone for the night, who would you be, Charlotte?"

"...C-can I be myself?" I ask, confused.

"No," they both say at once.

"Oh."

"I'd recommend a Charm name," Bella says. "No offense, but you can't pull off an Animal, Gemstone, or Sweet. Those are for girls who can play up the sex appeal and primal nature of what happens here."

"She could be a Girl Next Door?" Ruby offers. "I know you think they're boring but it's only for tonight, so..."

It... takes me a second. Not long, though. Like, um... three seconds? Ruby and Bella watch me, silent, waiting for me to answer this very important question. I never realized I needed a stripper name, but now that they've explained it all, it makes sense?

Like, um... if I'm introduced as Charlotte, that's... not very exciting, is it?

...To be fair I don't know if I'm usually very exciting, but tonight I'm trying my best and I want to be exciting for Hunter, so...

"I, um... I think... is..." I murmur, whispering the name on accident. "Is that okay?"

"Speak up," Bella says. "Be confident."

"S-sorry!" I mumble. "I just, um... Chantel?"

"Ooohhh!" Ruby squeals, hopping up and down, her barely there outfit not doing much to hold her in. "We have a new baby Exotic!"

"Stop using that term!" Bella snaps.

"Exotic Exotic Exotic!" Ruby says, giggling, hopping away

from Bella when she tries to smack her.

As annoyed as Bella looks, I think she's just pretending to be grumpy. She doesn't actually look that grumpy deep down. Her eyes are, um...

Giving up on whacking Ruby, she turns to me. "You sure that's it?"

"It's, um... the heroine of a romance story I'm writing?" I say. "Sometimes I like to pretend I'm her, or that I could be like her, so, um..."

"Okay," Bella says, nodding her approval. "Continue?"

"I love it already," Ruby croons.

"I share my story with Hunter. Um, he's my boyfriend. He's waiting out there. And I think he'd think it was... um... cute and funny and kind of sexy if... if that was my stripper name? So, um..."

"What about *you*?" Bella asks. "How would you feel going on stage like that? You have to *be* Chantel for the night, Charlotte. This isn't something you can half-ass. Go all the way or go home, got it?"

"I'd really like it, too," I say, nodding. "Um, sometimes Hunter and I roleplay and pretend we're the characters in my book and that's really fun, so..."

"Girl's kinky as hell, isn't she?" Crystal says, joining the conversation without being invited.

"...Oh gosh no," I mumble, cheeks burning bright red. "...I don't think so? Um..."

"Chantel it is," Bella says, standing tall, smiling at me. "Ladies!" she shouts to the rest of the dressing room. "Charlotte's gone. That name's dead to us here. Instead, let's welcome Chantel. She's only here for the night but I have a lot of faith in her. Fuck with her and I'll put itching powder in your favorite bra."

"That sounds awful," I say as everyone greets me as Chantel now.

Bella smirks. "It is. That's the point."

THE PERFECT PINK LIPSTICK

Episode 165

CHARLOTTE

Bella has her own private section in the stripclub changing room. It's blocked off with cubicle-style dividers and while it's not exactly quiet considering the noise the rest of the women make as they get ready for tonight's affairs, it's still nice to, um... just be somewhere that isn't right out in the open.

I'm nervous enough as it is and I'm really doing my best not to curl up in a ball or flee through the nearest fire escape, you know?

"So, *Chantel*," Bella says, sitting me down on a stool in front of a huge Hollywood-style makeup mirror. It has bright shining lightbulbs all around the outer edge, perfect for either seeing your own natural beauty or otherwise finding every single flaw possible on your face. It's both and this is the first time I've looked at myself in a mirror like this and I really don't think I like it very much because, um...

"Stop," Bella says, cutting me off as I press a finger against a spot on my face I never realized was there until now. "I'm in charge here. And what we're going to do is--"

"Blue and silver glitter eyeshadow!" Ruby gleefully announces as she invades Bella's personal workspace.

"Ruby," Bella says, flat, glaring at the Gemstone girl. "Go away."

"Nope, I'm helping," Ruby informs her. "Sorry, Bella! I promised the girls."

"You did not," Bella huffs. "But whatever. Fine. Get me the kit, please."

"On it!"

"Um, why blue and silver glitter eyeshadow?" I ask.

"Natural beauty is wonderful," Bella says, proud. "Even more so when you can bring it out in the real world. Except this isn't the real world. Everything in here needs to be played up and exaggerated. You can't just be beautiful, you need to be more than that. For some girls that means over the top colors, impossibly perfect shaded cheekbones that could never actually exist, and eyelashes out to here. For you, though..."

"I don't think I want eyelashes out to anywhere?" I say. "I have enough problems with mine as they are..."

"Got it!" Ruby says, jumping back into the thick of things, carrying a massive toolbox of a makeup kit in front of her.

It's probably more makeup than anyone in the world ever truly needs, except a girl can never have too much makeup, at least according to Jenny. I don't know which is the more correct statement right now, but I think Jenny might be wrong?

"We'll keep your jawline and cheekbones as is," Bella says, patting those spots with a makeup brush she's suddenly pulled out of nowhere. "It'll maintain your soft and innocent look. For your eyes, though. We really need them to pop. That's going to be your moneymaker tonight. Except I doubt the typical heavily sexed up bedroom smolder look won't work for you. So instead..."

"Blue and silver glitter," Ruby says, nodding. "What color

lipstick, though? Red's too extreme. Blue would match but it gives off more of a cold, calculating temptress look that I don't think quite works here. Hmm..."

"Figure it out while I finish the eyeshadow," Bella says, leaving it to her.

I didn't even realize we were starting already except suddenly Bella's poking and prodding me, pushing my chin and face in different directions, commanding me to close my eyes, then open them, look up, look down, look left, right, look deep inside yourself.

It takes me a second to realize her last request is a joke but when I do I giggle uncontrollably.

"It's not *that* funny," Bella says, flat, hiding a smirk.

"It's pretty funny, though," Ruby says, grinning at me.

"Time's up, Ruby. Lipstick. Color. Now. What do we have?"

Ruby nods to the stripper mistress of all things makeup. Slow, graceful, she reaches into the toolbox of a cosmetic kit and luxuriously pulls out--

"It's pink," Bella says, glancing at the lipstick, intrigued and perplexed. "Let me see."

"It's not *just* pink," Ruby tells her. "It's *mumble* pink. The perfect lightly blushed tone for whispering sweet nothings to your illicit lover, or in this case for that perfectly shy and innocent look that matches blue and silver glitter eyeshadow. Either one."

"I hate pink," Bella says, tipping my chin up. "It's cliche and overdone."

"I like pink?" I say, in case my opinion matters. I don't actually know right now.

"Quiet," Bella says, twisting the bottom of the lipstick, pushing the applicator out. "Let me see your lips."

I, um... I plump them up as best I can which I think is good enough because then Bella swipes the mumble pink lipstick across my top and bottom lips neatly, layering them with a perfectly light blushed pink color.

"Pout," Bella says. "Hurry up."

I do the lip thing Jenny taught me so I can make sure the color on my lips spreads evenly. Bella nods, fixes a little smudge with the very edge of her finger, and...

"Done," she says. "What do you think?"

"I think it's *great!*" Ruby says, ecstatic. "I mean, I *am* a color goddess though, so..."

"Ruby, shut up. Let Chantel take it all in. No more talking."

"Sorry, Bella!"

I, um... I've been sitting in front of the mirror this entire time but I kind of had other things on my mind? Mainly, if I can even do this, and how I really like the idea of blue and silver glittery eyeshadow but I just don't know if I'm the kind of girl who can pull off a look like that? Also Bella kept swiping this powder blush on my cheeks and I think I'm embarrassed enough as it is so I don't know if I need to look like I'm blushing even more, but...

As soon as I look in the mirror, someone else looks back at me.

"Oh wow," I say, staring at myself. "Ummmm..."

I move to touch my face to make sure that's me. Bella swats my hand away.

"No touching," she says, dictatorial. "Don't ruin my masterpiece."

"Okay," I say, agreeing with her.

"Pink though, am I right?" Ruby asks. "Huh, huh?"

"Yes, but I hate it," Bella lets her know.

"It's... wow!" I say, pursing my lips together, watching as the perfect pale blushed pink does its thing. I look like I'm about to kiss someone amazingly well for a very long time in the most passionate way possible and the lucky boy's name is Hunter Jackson and he's my stepbrother.

Seriously that's what I look like right now. I swear. I'm not just making that up for obvious reasons.

"Now..." Bella says, trailing off, grinning down at me.

I'm still seated on her stool in her private dressing room section and I think that means she gets to do whatever she wants with me to make me suitable for tonight.

I'm mostly fine with it. It's going really well so far.

"Outfit time!" Ruby gleefully says, clapping her hands together, hopping up and down.

"If you think the makeup looks good, you're gonna love her outfit," Bella says, snickering and winking at her Gemstone stripper friend.

"Heels?" Ruby asks. "Tell me there's heels, Bella."

"Obviously there's heels. Don't worry about that."

"Yay," I say, hopefully excited. "I'm so, um... I really am excited? I'm sorry, that sounded like I'm not excited, didn't it?"

"Charlotte doesn't exist anymore, Chantel," Bella says. "Let it all out, girl."

"Oh. Okay," I say, nodding. "Ummm... Yay! I... I'm r-really excited!"

"She's a work in progress," Ruby says, giggling. "So cute!"

"Go away, Ruby," Bella says, shooing her off. "We need to change."

All the other girls are already changing right outside, nothing doing, not a care in the world. Admittedly I was nervous I'd have to do the same? I'm, um... I've never changed in front of anyone before?

Except Hunter. I don't know if it counts. I've both taken my clothes off *and* put them on in front of him and that's, um... it's fine but also I still get embarrassed about it most of the time too, so...

It's just me and Bella this time, though.

I think that's supposed to make this easier but it's not actually?

JENNY

There's some things in life you need to experience firsthand to fully understand. This is one of those things.

"Alright, babes!" Angela says, cheerfully encouraging us as our confused Uber driver pulls up outside the Paper Slipper stripclub. "We need to start this off on the right foot. All of us, and yes, I totally mean *all of us,* need to strut our stuff straight to the front door, march out cute booties in there like there's no tomorrow, and show the world what we're made of."

"Um, like, what *are* we made of, though?" Clarissa asks, which is probably not as philosophical as it sounds.

"Ninety-nine percent of the human body is hydrogen, oxygen, carbon, and nitrogen," I say, being a smart ass. "Mostly in water form."

"Wait, really?" Angela asks, intrigued. "Huh! The more you know. I was going to say, like, sugar and spice and everything sexy and awesome, but that's really cool, Jenny!"

"Thanks," I say, laughing. Seriously, I love the cheerleaders. They're so amazing.

I'm not even joking. They're like my best friends now. Love you, babes!

Anyways, um... besides that we have one minor issue, which is--

"I don't want to ruin the plan," my brother says, chiming in, sitting next to Angela in the backseat. "But, uh... am I supposed to strut, too? I'm a guy, not a babe."

"Teddy, you're *totally* a babe," Angela says, making eyes at him.

I don't know what kind of eyes those are, but I don't like them. Something's going on there, I swear. I have no idea what yet, though. Ugh.

"Aw, thanks," Teddy says, clueless.

"You can totally swagger instead, though," Angela adds.

"That makes more sense, right? Like, girls strut and boys swagger. There's only one of you, but if there were more boys, you'd swagger together. Just, um... this is kind of our night so is it alright if you stand behind us while we strut first? It'll, like, totally be worth it, I promise."

I think she winks at him but I'm sitting up front with the driver and I wasn't paying attention for a second so I don't know for sure.

Seriously what the heck is going on there?

Knowing Teddy, probably nothing, but...

"I don't want to be rude, but I have another ride scheduled," our Uber driver says. "Your plan sounds solid, though. Strut and swagger away, my friends."

"Thanks!" Clarissa beams. "You're so nice. Totally giving you five-stars, by the way."

"I do my best," the woman says, nodding to her through the rearview mirror.

I help myself out of the car. Teddy holds the door open for not only Angela but also Clarissa. Angela holds her hand out for some reason and Teddy takes it, helping her up? Come on, guys...

Whatever. It's not important. Now it's *on.* It's game time, baby!

Angela and Clarissa step up to the plate, taking a spot on either side of me. Teddy holds up the rear, ready for action.

And... *go!*

We strut. Heck yeah! I strut my little butt off and, um... the cheerleaders do the same. Angela's really working it, actually. Goddamn, you go, girl.

...I belatedly realize that with Teddy standing behind us he has a perfect view of exactly what she's bouncing back at him and I don't know how I feel about that...

In, like, twenty seconds our strutting pays off as we get to the front door of the stripclub with power, poise, and total babeworthy hotness. Aw yeah!

"Ladies," the burly bouncer says as we approach. "Looking good."

"Like, thanks," Angela says, tossing her long blonde hair over her shoulder. "But I almost have a boyfriend, so, like..."

"Wait, you do?" I ask, confused. "Who?"

"Oh, um... you don't know him, don't even worry about it, Jenny."

"Do I know him?" Clarissa asks, confused.

"No, um... babes, I was just, like, saying it, that's all."

"I'm not sure if I know him either?" Teddy says, which is apparently the wrong thing to say because Angela looks really deflated now. Disappointed, even?

Hmmmmmm...

"Teddy, you *do* know him, but let's not talk about this right now, okay?" Angela says, hushed and hurried. "Right, so, babes..."

"We're here... *to dance!*" Clarissa informs the bouncer, flashing him a quick cheer move to prove she means business.

"And I'm here to check your IDs," the bouncer says, a hint of a smirk tugging at his lips.

"Oh, right, I totally have one of those," Clarissa says, which doesn't sound suspicious at all...

I don't know how we're going to get away with this.

We each take out our fake IDs. Thankfully that part works. I was worried one or the other of the cheerleaders would forget and hand over their real IDs, but, well... so far so good. Even Teddy remembers to use his and I was even more worried about that. My brother hates lying, or, um... it's probably more accurate to say he *can't* lie. He's just really really bad at it.

This is why I'm suspicious but also kind of not? I think if he were hiding something he would've given himself away already. Hmmmm...

"Right this way," the buff bouncer says, holding the door

open with one hand, handing our IDs back with the other, fanned out like playing cards.

We each take our respective fakes, which thankfully worked, and then, um...

I forgot we were supposed to keep strutting into the stripclub after that but the cheerleaders remember for me. They do it really well, too. I end up holding back on accident, strutless, and Teddy walks alongside me. His eyes are--

Teddy!

"Excuse you!" I hiss at him as he stares at Angela's butt.

"What!" Teddy snaps back, as usual.

"Are you staring at Angela's butt?"

I said that a little too loud apparently. Angela heard me.

"Like, oh my gosh! Teddy! Were you staring at my butt?!" she asks, excitedly scandalized.

"I was actually looking at the carpet?" Teddy says, perplexed. "I don't know why, but I imagined something different? I mean, now that we're here, I think it works. But for some reason I thought there'd be wood paneling instead of plush red carpet, you know?"

"Oh," Angela says, deflated again. I almost feel bad for her now. "I mean, once you're done looking at the carpet, do you *want* to stare at my butt for a little bit? Because we still have some strutting left to do and I'm really proud of the progress I've been making with my squats lately."

"Sure?"

"Okay!"

...Guys, come on, what the heck...

I don't even know if I can blame my brother for staring at Angela's butt, either. She's clearly got a nice rear end. I mean, I get it, Teddy. I'm not happy about it, but as long as it's just the occasional admiration glance or two, it's fine. Maybe. I'm conflicted.

Anyways, before I can figure out how much I hate the fact

that my brother's about to stare at my friend's butt after she just asked him if he would, um...

There. Right the freak there. Is Hunter. He's sitting at a table, regular chairs on one side and a high-backed booth on the other.

He's in the booth seat. And he is *not* alone. He's with a stripper.

I don't want to be too judgmental about it but she's just kind of obviously a stripper, you know? She's got the silvery blue glittery makeup going on, the total sexy stripper look, and while she's wearing a robe for the most part, there's a hint of what's underneath peeking through and it's totally stripper-worthy is all I'm going to say about that.

Dude, you're supposed to be with Charlotte, buddy!

"Excuse you!" I say, marching up to him to give him a piece of my mind. You're in for it now, buddy. Ugh. Boys. Am I right? "What do you think you're--"

HUNTER

"Sorry," I brusquely say to the stripper who sits in my booth with me. "I'm sure you're great or whatever, but I'm here with my girlfriend, so..."

There. I did it. Crisis averted or something like that. Also holy fucking shit, this stripper is hot as hell. I've only barely glanced at her out of the corner of my eye but she's everything I could ever want in a stripper, if, uh... you know, I ever wanted a stripper?

I mean, yes, I wrote about my badass noir detective dude going to a stripclub for Baby Sis, and I guess he probably would've hooked up with strippers if he wasn't super into the girl behind the bar, and if he *did* happen to hook up with a stripper she'd look *exactly* like the one sitting next to me in the booth right now who apparently hasn't taken a hint because

STEPBROTHER, PLEASE STOP TEASING ME!

instead of leaving she's still sitting there, waiting for me to look at her.

Anyways, point being, I'm not going to be that guy who randomly falls in love with a stripper, alright? I have a girlfriend, she's amazing, and--

Also where the fuck is everyone? I don't know how long I've been waiting in the showroom, but I kind of figured the guys would be here by now, or at least Baby Sis would be back after hanging out with her stripper friend which is a thing I never thought would happen in a million years.

So yeah, that's where I'm at and also I make the sudden bad decision to actually acknowledge the stripper sitting next to me with my eyes instead of grunting and hoping she goes away on her own.

And... holy fucking shit, she's as hot as I thought she was. Hotter, actually. Fuck me, man...

It helps that she's my stepsister and not actually a stripper unless you count tonight's amateur night competition.

"Um, hi," Baby Sis mumbles, blinking at me a million times a second. "Is... is this seat t-taken...?"

"Fuck no it's not," I say, faster than fast. "Take it. Please."

"I'm, um... I'm Chantel..." she whispers, which I think is supposed to sound anxious but the way she says it is seductive as fuck.

I want her in my lap immediately, and not just because there's a sign off to the side that says *"This way to the private rooms"* with an arrow and a shadowy silhouette of a girl giving a dude a lap dance and everything.

"Are you now?" I ask, smirking back at her. "Did you pick that name yourself?"

"Shhhhh!" Baby Sis says, placing a single finger against my lips. "You're, um... you're supposed to pretend, alright?"

"Oh, yeah, sure," I say, trying not to laugh. "Got it. So, Chantel... what brings you here?"

Just to backtrack for a second, the outfit that's really fucking with my head right now is:

First off, I should clarify that she's wearing a satin black robe so it's not like she's on show for the entire club to see. It's basically just me because she's facing my way and the front of the robe is open enough for me to get a perfect view of exactly what's going on underneath.

And what's beneath the robe is this stupidly hot little black dress that looks like it was custom-made to fit her body and hers alone. It's got this wrap-around sleeveless halter-style thing going on, with a teardrop-shaped cutout showcasing her cleavage. It's shaped in such a way that not only do I get a perfect peek of the upper and inner curves of her breasts, but it tugs them apart slightly, showing off the girls even more. Fuck, I want to bury my face between her breasts like they're the sexiest pillow known to man.

Anyways, not to get too distracted but the rest of the dress is sexy as hell, too. I don't know what the fuck is going on exactly but there's these, like... asymmetrical? Let's go with that. I don't even know if that's a thing, but it is now. The design of the dress has cut-out sections, showing off a flash of bare skin here and there, but instead of being in the same places on either side of the dress it's more like they show up in both the best and least likely spots possible.

I can see the opposite side of one breast; the outer curve plus a peek at some high quality underboob. If I tilt my head to the side, just so, I can see her bare hip flashing through another cut-out that slides halfway down her waist. The dress is still a dress so it has to stop at some point, but it's basically the miniest of fucking mini-dresses and I'm pretty sure if she bends over she'll be showing off every single inch of her panties, so...

To top it all off, there's a inch or two of bare skin immediately under the bottom hem of the dress, tantalizing and sweet, and then matching black cut out leggings that go from mid-thigh to her ankle. They cover the front of her leg just fine, but on either side, inside and out, they have a similar asymmetrical cutaway pattern going on where, like... it's just all leg as far as the eye can see. She's both covered and not covered at the same time.

...I didn't know anything like this existed and I'm absolutely loving it, holy fucking shit...

"...Do you like it?" she asks, and I think she probably said more before that but I've been busy staring her up and down. "It's, um... it's really comfortable?"

"Look," I say, straight to the point. "Not only do I like it, but I'm pretty sure I'd blow through about ten-thousand dollars begging you for lap dances if I had that much, so..."

"Really?!" she asks, excited. "Um, don't do that, though. I'll, um... I don't know how it works but I'll give you one for free?"

"Dude, what kind of stripper are you?" I ask, laughing.

"I'm, um... I'm a one man only kind of stripper and t-tag, you're it..." she says, nervously tapping the side of my arm.

"That was the best and the worst pickup line I've ever heard in my life," I tell her.

"Oh," she says, shifty-eyed. "Did it work, though?"

"Yes. I'm yours. You win."

"Yay!"

It's at this point that Teddy's Little Sister marches her annoying ass up to my table, points at me like I'm a flagrant criminal, one who definitely hates puppies and Christmas or something, and says:

"Excuse you! What do you think you're--"

Then she stops. Blinks. Baby Sis shyly waves at Jenny while hurrying to pull her robe shut to cover up. Angela and Clarissa strut their stupidly pert cheerleader asses over to the table like they own the place, which they don't, sorry. And my best bro Teddy walks over, goofy smile on his face, waving at my stepsister.

"Hey, Baby Charlie," he says. "Wow, you look great! That's a really cool look. I like the blue eyeshadow."

"Thanks, Teddy!" Baby Sis says, excited. "Um, my... I don't know if she's my friend, actually? Bella. I think maybe she's my friend but I don't know yet. She did it for me."

"That's awesome," Teddy says, nodding back.

"What about my makeup, Teddy?" Angela asks him, anything but subtle.

"I thought you said on the drive over you weren't done with yours yet?" Teddy says.

"Oh, um, I mean, right, but how's it look right now?"

"Your makeup always looks really nice," he says, sincere. "I like it."

I don't know how or why that works, but it does, and I end up witnessing what happens when a girl's panties melt, except I really don't want to. Go melt your fucking panties for Teddy elsewhere, Angela. Fuck.

As if this is the cue for everyone else to just cut into my alone time with Baby Sis, some dark redhead stripper zooms up out of nowhere with a clipboard and paperwork. Clarissa sees her first and starts to squeal, then Angela realizes who it is and does the same. The stripper also starts to squeal exactly like the cheerleaders and it's kind of weird at first but then somehow it makes perfect sense because--

"Ruby!" Clarissa squeals, squealing more. "Like, oh my gosh, you're so pretty!"

"Aw, girl, you too!" Ruby says back to her. "My girls! You made it! I'm so excited. I couldn't be prouder!"

"Totally!" Angela gushes. "Like, Ruby, oh my gosh, you're so inspiring! We still talk about you at practice. It's, like, totally inspirational."

"Awwww, don't, you're going to make me blush!" Ruby says, but I don't think anything in the entire world could make this woman blush.

They come together in some kind of group hug that also

involves jumping in a circle and, excuse me, ladies, this is a stripclub. What the fuck is going on here?

"Oh oh oh, before I forget," Ruby says, tapping the papers and clipboard she's now holding against her chest. "Fill these out, okay? You need to hand them in at the bar before amateur night starts or you won't be able to join the competition. Very important, alright? And then, like, can I help you with your makeup? Bella and I did Chantel already. She's so cute, isn't she?"

"Um, who's Chantel?" Clarissa asks, glancing around, looking for her.

"Do we even know a Chantel?" Angela adds, equally confused.

"I'm Chantel?" Baby Sis says, lifting her hand in the air, awkward.

Clarissa and Angela stare at her, baffled.

"Babes, I think it's her secret stripper name," Jenny says, finally helping out. "Also, I love it! What a cute name, Charl--" she starts, then stops and fixes it. "I mean, Chantel. That's going to take getting used to."

"Oh my gosh I want a stripper name!" Clarissa says, as if the idea never dawned on her.

"Same, babe. Same," Angela agrees. "Let's, like, totally think about what our stripper names will be while letting Ruby turn us into the hottest hotties possible, alright?"

"Okay!"

And, uh... that's how I end up sitting in a stripclub booth with my stepsister, Teddy, and his little sister, while the cheerleaders rush out back to figure out their stripper names and get stripper makeup done and, look... I don't know what else I can't get the image of Baby Sis in her dropdead fucking little black dress out of my head.

One thing, though:

Where the hell did she get it and how'd she keep it a secret for this long?

Anyways, everything's going great until I remember the reason we're here in the first place...

My evil ex-girlfriend parades through the front door, shaking every possible curve in her body, trying to pull all eyes in the stripclub towards her. It's annoying as fuck, especially because a lot of the random dudes in the place actually look, as if they're seriously interested in her arrival.

Erica scans the showroom as if surveying her domain, pretending she's the Queen of everything. Her eyes stop on me and she prances over, practically skipping with excitement.

"Huntsy, you're here!"

Fuck.

166

HELPING HANNAH

Episode 166

CHARLOTTE

Hunter and I are cuddling and talking with Jenny and Teddy when suddenly Erica shows up.

I mean, um... I knew she was coming because that's kind of what the point of tonight was. She texted me earlier with vague threats about how I probably shouldn't even come if I know what's good for me, too. I tried asking what she meant and she just replied with:

ERICA (WHY IS SHE SO MEAN?)

"YOU KNOW WHAT I MEAN, CHARLOTTE!
IF THAT'S EVEN YOUR REAL NAME!"

I still have no idea why she thinks that's not my real name? It's very confusing.

Anyways, so, yes...

"Huntsy, you're here!" Erica screeches, sashaying over to our table. "You'll be leaving with *me* tonight, by the way. I mean, once you see me on stage I'm sure you'll realize who the better stepsister is and we can put all this silly competition nonsense aside. I'm only doing it to make sure that girl pretending to be your stepsister knows her place. It's getting a bit tiring though, don't you think?"

She fakes a yawn, holding her hand over her mouth. Hunter glares at her, brow furrowed, as if she may be slightly unhinged. She's very confident, at least? I, um... I don't really know what else to say.

If you don't have anything nice to say, you shouldn't say anything at all, right?

"I know we're in a stripclub, but you don't have to spend time with the strippers, Huntsy," Erica says, casually looking my way before tossing her hair over her shoulder with a haughty huff. "Shoo shoo, you can leave now, honey."

Before I can respond, except I honestly don't know how to respond, suddenly Lance shows up. He hops through the front door, scans the room quick, looking for Erica, and when he finally finds her he jogs over.

"Sorry about that!" Lance says, apologetic. "The guy out front was asking me a lot of questions. Did he do that to you guys, too? I don't know what that was about. I know I look young for my age and, uh... you know, nevermind. We're not supposed to say this out loud, are we?"

He looks at the ID in his hand, which I'm assuming is fake like the rest of ours? Then he pulls his wallet out of his pocket, slips the ID back in, and pockets it again.

"You idiot," Erica says, glaring at him. "I *told* you what to say and you *still* almost blew it. Luckily my rival in love doesn't seem to be here yet so it's fine. Is she even coming? Did I already win? I don't know why I bothered if that's the case, but, well... I'll still dance for you, Huntsy baby. Don't you worry about that..."

She winks at him and Hunter's not even paying attention now, which, um... if she notices she doesn't seem to care that much?

"Uh, she's right there, though?" Lance says, looking at me, confused.

"Who?" Erica asks.

"Charlotte?" he offers, nodding at me, then kind of pointing but I think he feels bad because pointing's impolite, you know? He jerks his head slightly and waves to me instead after.

"Hi Lance," I say, smiling and waving back. "I'm, um... I'm Chantel tonight, okay? It's my name for amateur night."

"Gotcha," he says, keeping my secret safe. "That's cool."

"Excuse you, but don't ogle my stepsister like that," Hunter grunts at him. "Thanks."

"Wait, *what?*" Erica asks, gasping hard. She stares at Lance, then Hunter, then me. It takes her a second of squinting to, um... I don't actually know what she's doing but when she's done doing it she points a long, neatly manicured, freshly painted nailed finger at me. "*You!*" she demands. "I *knew* it! Chantel, is it? Is *that* your real name? What are you hiding from my darling Huntsy and why are you trying so hard to steal him away from me, you harlot?"

"It's... it's a stage name!" I protest. "Bella and Ruby said I needed a stripper name and I g-got to pick it so, um... I like the name Chantel? I think it's nice. Ruby says I'm an Exotic now? B-but--"

"What the *hell* is an Exotic?" Erica asks. "Who's Bella? And Ruby? What's going on here?"

"*I'm* Bella," Bella says, strutting over. "Is everything alright, Chantel?" she asks, smiling sweetly.

"You're a stripper," Erica says, catching on quick.

It kind of helps that Bella's provocatively dressed in, um... it's barely anything and she looks really nice now and oh my gosh I could never wear an outfit like that.

A pair of sheer stockings with a baby pink line on either side, inside and out, cling to her toned legs, a matching pink bow circling the top of either side of the stockings. A garter belt connects her stockings to her pale pink panties, which, um... they're panties and that's it. Another pink bow sits at the top of the middle of her panties, just below her belly button or right above her, um... *you know...* as if she's a present ready to be unwrapped by a generous man with the right amount of money in his wallet.

Her top's a little less revealing but not by much. It's, um... a corset-style bra, pushing her breasts up high, cleavage out to here. Her toned stomach peeks through the bottom, another matching pink bow neatly tying it all together, but this one's actually functional and I'm pretty sure if she were to pull the ribbons the entire top would come undone, falling off.

I think that's the point, actually? It's very impressive and functional.

Also she looks so pretty. I wonder if I could pull off an outfit like that? Like, um... n-not right now, but... for Hunter? In private? Later?

I imagine wearing that for him and watching excitedly as he tugs the ribbon of my corset, unraveling the whole thing, setting me loose, a perfectly wrapped and now unwrapped present to end a special date night...

Oh gosh, yes please.

Anyways, um... Erica's angrily glaring at Bella and Bella's having none of it.

"You're the attempted man thief, are you?" Bella asks.

"I am *not* a man-thief, thank you very much!" Erica snaps. "Not that I have to defend myself to you, you... you... it's too impolite to say in front of Huntsy. I can't do it."

"You want me to have her kicked out?" Bella asks, nodding to me.

"Um, no, I need to go against her in amateur night," I say, because I'm still determined to do my best and fight for Hunter.

"Ha!" Erica scoffs. "I knew it. I knew you'd resort to cheating if you could. As if! I'm not scared of, well...

whatever's going on here? You think I'd be afraid of your little pink hussy friend, *Chantel*? Never."

"Boys," Bella says, seductively sweet, talking to the boys now, ignoring Erica entirely. "Can I get you some drinks?"

Hunter tries to order a beer and Bella knocks that back, shaking her head, knowing his secret. He reluctantly accepts the offer of a non-alcoholic drink that potentially looks like a cocktail. Teddy wants that, too. Lance goes with a Sprite instead.

"How about you, darling?" Bella asks me. "I have something in mind if you're up for it. Girls drink free."

"Um, okay," I say, smiling.

Even if I'm a girl and she's a girl, um... the way she's looking at me right now, I can see why guys like her. She's very good at this. I feel like I need to take notes but I didn't bring a notebook and I left my phone with my regular clothes in the dressing room.

"We're *not* staying," Erica huffs as soon as Bella leaves. "*Lance!* Come!"

"Don't forget the form!" I call out, peeling off one of the amateur night submission forms on the clipboard in front of me. "You have to fill it out and hand it in at the bar to enter the contest."

"I already *know* that, you idiot!" Erica puffs, snatching the form out of my hand without a second thought. "You think you're all that just because you know some stupid stripper. Ugh! People like you infuriate me. I can't wait to destroy you and claim what's mine."

Erica stomps off, heading to an empty table as far away from me as possible. It's near the stage that, um... I think her name's Gia but I haven't actually met her yet. Anyways, she's dancing nearby and she keeps winking at Lance, who, um... he seems to enjoy the winking, so I guess that's good?

"What a bitch," Jenny grumbles as soon as Erica's gone.

"I didn't know you knew a stripper," Teddy says to me. "She seems nice."

"She is!" I say, excited. "Um, she helped me pick my outfit for tonight? It's a secret, though. I'm wearing it under my robe. It's, um... it's kind of embarrassing but it's good for pole dancing and--"

"It's hot as fuck," Hunter says, smirking. "Goddamn, Baby Sis..."

"I want to see~!" Jenny whines. "Ugh. I wish we'd gotten here a couple minutes sooner. Sorry for accusing you of chatting it up with a stripper by the way, Hunter. You just look so good, Charlotte! Seriously, what the heck, girl. Where'd the makeup come from?"

Bella struts over with our drinks on a tray and starts handing them out. She makes it look so easy and sensual and I have no idea how she does it like that but it's clear she's a professional.

"Who's this?" Bella asks me, subtly nodding towards Jenny.

"This is my friend," I tell her. "Jenny. Um, Jenny, this is Bella. I met her at, um... that place we went with the cheerleaders and... the cheerleader discount?"

I know I shouldn't be embarrassed about it but I'm just kind of nervous talking about a high-end lingerie shop in front of Hunter and Teddy...

"Huh?" Jenny asks, confused. "Oh! Wait! I remember! Oh my gosh, you went on your own? *Charlotte!* You saucy little minx. Wow. Seriously, wow. I'm proud, don't get me wrong. I just, you know... I didn't think you had it in you?"

"It was really hard," I admit. "But Saskia and Bella were super nice and helped me. It wasn't as bad as I thought it'd be."

"Chantel's a natural," Bella says, winking.

"Oh, right, you're Chantel tonight. Shoot. I need a stripper name too, don't I?"

76

"Do you?" Teddy asks, concerned. "I know you're here to have fun with Baby Chantel and your friends, but I don't know if I can call you by a stripper name, Jenny. It's kind of weird."

"Who's this?" Bella asks, turning on the charm and favoring Teddy with a smolderingly seductive grin. "Not anyone's boyfriend, I assume? He's *very* cute..."

"That's my brother," Jenny groans. To Teddy, she adds, "Look, I get it, alright? But if everyone else has a stripper name I definitely need a stripper name. Just deal with it, alright?"

"Ah, the brother," Bella says, somehow turning her smolder even higher. "If you want, I can take care of him for tonight. Have you been in one of the private rooms yet, baby? There's this song I'd love to show you. It *really* does it for me if you know what I mean. I only share it with men I find especially interesting and I have to admit, you're definitely my type, so... what do you think?"

Jenny gapes. Hunter snickers. Teddy looks slightly confused but maybe?

"Sure?" he offers.

"Have you had a chance to stop by the ATM yet?" Bella asks. "It's cash only, baby. Don't worry, I'll give you the friends and family discount. Since you're Jenny's brother, it's only fair, right...?"

"Go for it, dude," Hunter says, full on laughing now. "Damn."

"We're supposed to get money out for the competition anyways, right?" Teddy says with a shrug.

"Teddy!" Jenny whines. "What the heck."

"What! I didn't even do anything," Teddy counters. "I'm trying to help."

"Oh, don't worry, I'll help you, handsome," Bella says, taking Teddy's hand and tugging him out of the booth.

"*Teddy!*" Jenny yells as he leaves with Bella. "You know

what? Nevermind. I give up. I'm done. He'll figure it out on his own."

"It's okay," I tell her. "Bella's really nice. I'm sure the song she wants to share with Teddy will be good. Don't worry."

"...Dude," Hunter says, staring at me. "Are you serious right now?"

"Um, dude," I say, because I thought I was. "Yes?"

"So, I, um... I don't want to ruin this for you, Charlotte..." Jenny says, conflicted. "But when Bella said she has a song she wants to share with him, I think what she really meant is she's going to give him a lap dance? In a private room, you know?"

...*What*...

I, um... oh gosh, I thought it was actually about a song. I don't know why. I probably should've realized. I mean, Bella *is* a stripper and she's working tonight, so, um...

"...Oh..." I murmur, hoping my cheeks aren't too red right now. I know they are but I'm just kind of hoping they aren't, you know?

Also a couple seconds later, Angela and Clarissa come back. They look mostly the same but also kind of different. I can tell it's them, but oh wow, their makeup is amazing. Ruby clings to their side, trying not to squeal with excitement. It's not really working.

The cheerleaders have matching outfits, but different colors. Angela's wearing a super short purple latex skirt with a matching, um... it's like a tube top but it only covers her boobs? It looks like it's about to fall off, but so far it's managed to cling on for dear life. Clarissa's is the same, except orange. They both have faux fur trim at the top of their tube tops and the bottom of their skirts, giving them a wild primal look. The fur is purple or orange depending on the girl, too.

Ruby did their makeup the opposite colors, so, um... Clarissa has bright purple eyeshadow with pale blue sparkles and Angela's is orange. Angela has tiger stripes in hers, though? It's kind of amazing and looks really fun and I hope she likes it a lot.

"Like, babes," Angela says, shifting side to side, modeling for us. "What do you think? *Totally,* am I right?"

"Totally!" Clarissa says, hopping up and down, nearly falling out of her top.

"Love it, babes," Jenny says, offering her nod of approval.

"You both look so pretty!" I say, excited. "I like it."

"Aw, that's so nice, Chantel!" Angela says, giggly. "Ruby reminded us to call you that. Love it, by the way! Same, Jenny. Love you both, babes!"

"What's with the tiger stripes?" Hunter asks, head cocked to the side.

"It's to, like, go with my stripper name," Angela says, tossing her blonde hair over her shoulder. "Tonight I'm... Bastet! She's, like, totally an Egyptian goddess of all the kitties. Which, alright, so this is a *stretch,* but, like... *kitty,* you know? The one down there. Totally, babes. I'm the goddess of *that* tonight. *Me~ow!*"

"I like it," I say, blushing hard. "It's, um... does that mean you're an Animal name, then?"

"Definitely an Animal!" Ruby squeals, excited. "So proud of my girls."

"I'm Desire!" Clarissa says, jumping and clapping. I'm really worried about her top but it's performing admirably thus far.

"A Charm!" I say, excited. "It's a really pretty name, too."

"I thought we could all, like, pick one of each, right?" Clarissa explains. "So, like, you're an Exotic, right, Charlie? Sorry! Chantel. And, you know, I'm a Charm, and Bastet is an Animal, so..."

"I have no idea what any of that means," Jenny says, glancing at each of us as if we're speaking another language. "What kind of name do I go with then?"

"There's, um... Gemstones, Sweets, and Girls Next Door left," I tell her.

"Don't pick a Girl Next Door name," Ruby says. "Bella will hate it."

"Ugh, tell me about it," Jenny says with a sigh. "I already *have* a girl next door name and, alright... I like my name, don't get me wrong, but everyone always thinks it's so nice and wholesome and whatever. I'm not *always* nice and wholesome, you know?"

"What's the opposite of nice and wholesome, though?" Clarissa asks, nose scrunched up.

"I... I don't know... let me think..." Jenny says, equally confused for a second. "Oh oh oh, I know! Guys. How about..." She pauses for emphasis. "Cherry. But not *just* Cherry! Cherry *Delight!*"

"Yes! Totally, Jenny!"

"Love it, babe," Angela agrees. "You rock. And with some hot red lipstick? Totally."

"I don't want to say this is right up my alley, but my name *is* Ruby, so..." Ruby says, grinning conspiratorially at Jenny.

"I'm in," she says. "Whatever it is, I don't even care. I'll do it."

"That's the spirit!"

Ruby's about to steal Jenny away for a stripper makeover except Angela has one last pressing question before she goes:

"Um, where'd Teddy go by the way?" she asks.

"Ugh, don't even get me started," Jenny grumbles. "I mean, look, I get it, this is a stripclub, and she really *did* seem nice, but... my brother's oblivious sometimes, you know?"

"Um, what?" Angela asks, eyes wide, starting to panic.

"Bella said she had a nice song she wanted to show him and... she took him?"

"*Ohhhhhhh,*" Ruby fawns, giggling. "Private room?"

"Yeah," Hunter says, rolling his eyes.

"Sounds fun."

"Wait, *what!*" Angela blinks, looks down the hall leading to the private rooms, and gapes, open-mouthed, just staring off into the dark empty hallway leading to, um...

I don't actually know what happens in private rooms but it's a stripclub, so...

I hope Teddy's having a nice time, at least?

Angela looks like she feels the opposite way.

One by one, group by group, everyone else arrives shortly after.

First the romance book club girls show up, all of them nervously glancing around the stripclub showroom with a mix of awe, interest, and illicit curiosity. Joanna pops over to say hi and the other girls swarm behind her, waving excitedly and complimenting me on, um... I'm wearing the robe now because I don't think I can walk around in the open with what I'm wearing underneath. I'd be way too embarrassed.

...I'm supposed to dance in this later...

I feel like that's the easy part, though? It's, um... it's not that it's *easy*, b-but it's easier than walking around like this, because maybe people will be more focused on my dancing than my outfit and the entire point of amateur night is the dancing, so, um...

There's a surprise for that, too. I hope I can pull it off. My cheeks hurt already just thinking about it but if I'm dancing then, um... maybe people won't notice me blushing?

...Bella promised me it'd be amazing and she'd help me if I needed anything, so...

"We'll grab a booth," Joanna says, smiling kindly at me. "Come join us later, *Chantel*," she adds, winking as she uses my *nom de plume* for the night. "We found a novella online that takes place in a stripclub so we're going to read it while

81

we wait and have a quickie book club discussion if you want to hang out with us after."

"Okay!" I say, excited. I'm going to miss book clubs over summer break. "Um, wait, H-Hunter, do you want to, um...?"

"Yeah," he says, grinning and sidling close. He wraps his arm around me, both protective and possessive. I kind of love it.

Next up are Sam, Chloe, and Amelia, who all come in side by side. Admittedly Sam and Chloe look fine but Chloe has to practically drag Amelia into the stripclub by force, linking their arms together and pulling her inside. Sam waves to the boys and Chloe waves to me and Amelia starts to kind of wave except before she knows what's going on Chloe drags her into the middle of the club and they start dancing their butts off.

It's not stripper dancing, it's regular dancing. Chloe seems really into it. Amelia? Um, not so much, but Chloe's excitement is apparently infectious and Amelia forgets where she is after a little while and starts giggling and trying to copy Chloe. Chloe laughs and helps her figure out some good moves. A few newcomers to the club, mostly men, blink at the girls who definitely aren't strippers but are still dancing, as if they aren't entirely sure what to make of them.

"Hey," Sam says, coming over to say hi for a second. "Gotta keep up with the girls, but just wanted to wish you luck, Chantel. You got this!"

"Thank you, Sam," I say, beaming. "Wait, um... how'd you know my name?"

Instead of answering, he just winks at me and then heads over to dance with Chloe and Amelia even though I'm really not sure this is that kind of club.

And, um... last but not least are--

Hannah and Oliver...

They step through the front doors, awkward and silent. Hannah stumbles on the carpet as if she's forgotten how to walk. Oliver blinks and peers around, looking for something that may not even be here. It's a very confused and disoriented look. Hannah and Oliver look at each other for a second, which I think they both decide was an accident or a mistake because they immediately snap their eyes away from making direct contact and stare at anything but each other afterwards.

"Okay, uh, what the fuck?" Hunter says, watching the two of them ever so slowly make their way further and further into the stripclub.

"I, um... excuse me..." I mumble, scooting out of the booth and scurrying over to Hannah. I take her hand fast and pull her away before even saying hi.

Oliver furrows his brow, watching me borrow his rideshare mate. I... I wave. Very badly. He... waves back, also maybe badly but I don't stick around long enough to figure it out.

Also I have no idea where else to go so I kind of accidentally drag Hannah down the hallway towards the private rooms. Like, um, for lap dances, right? Bella said we could use the rooms tonight but we need to talk to some man first and admittedly I didn't think this all the way through when I started doing it but I'm here now and it's too late to turn back, you know?

"Um, hi," I mumble to a man sitting behind a small counter with a plastic barrier and a small hole at the bottom, presumably for, you know, handing over money for whatever?

...Yes, that's probably how paying for lap dances works, Charlotte...

I'm very bad at this. Oh gosh.

"You're Bella's girl, right?" he asks, scrutinizing me. "What's up?"

"Um, c-can we use a room please?" I ask.

"Wait, huh?" Hannah says, startled. "I..."

"Is this a lap dance thing or a girl talk thing?" the guy asks, rolling his eyes at me.

"Girl talk thing?" I offer, hopeful.

He shrugs. "Sure, it's quiet. Down that hall, second from the last door on the left, alright? But look, no offense, I get that you're Bella's work in progress or whatever, but usually you're supposed to pay. And you generally tip your friends, too. Understand?"

"Charlotte, we really don't have to--" Hannah starts to say but I cut her off awkwardly.

Mainly by, um... reaching for my pocket which usually has a little bit of money in it except I realize I don't have pockets right now and I'm wearing a robe and barely anything underneath so this is just really bad and I feel bad and I'm supposed to give this man money but I don't have money, so...

Suddenly Natalie appears from out of nowhere. She smoothly walks up to the counter, step by step, small, light, and compelling. She nods curtly to the man behind the counter, who looks equally confused to see her. Without a word, she pulls twenty dollars from a professional looking mustard yellow leather clutch handbag hanging from a thin chain strapped around her shoulder. She hands the money to the man, who accepts it, bewildered.

"For them," Natalie says. "Now if you could please tell me where the clueless boy and the busty blonde cheerleader in purple latex are, I'd appreciate it."

"Can't let you back there," he says. "Private means private. Whatever happens happens. I'm sure you understand."

Without a word, Natalie reaches into her clutch again and produces a fifty dollar bill, sliding it across the counter through the small plastic hole.

"You can knock, but that's it," he says, smirking. "No going in. If they don't answer, it's not my problem. Middle door on the right."

"Understood. Thank you," Natalie says, nodding politely, turning towards the private room hallway. "Chantel, Hannah," she adds, favoring us with a slightly more congenial nod. "Let's talk later, shall we?"

"Um, okay?" I say, slightly puzzled. I don't think anyone invited Natalie, but I can't exactly say I'm entirely surprised she's here either if that makes sense?

"Who's Chantel, though?" Hannah asks, also confused but for a different reason.

"Um, me Kind of? Hold on, um..."

I grab her hand and hurry down the hall past Natalie, who's about to knock and request to speak with Teddy and Angela and, um... I think that's it but I don't know how big the rooms are so maybe there's more people in there?

...How do private rooms for lap dances even work, really?

I'm about to find out...

I push open the door and pull Hannah in with me and--

Oh.

There's a cushioned bench on one side and a pair of speakers playing the same music that's blasting in the club, just slightly louder since it's a private, contained room. And that's it. Honestly I don't know what more I expected.

Hannah and I stare at the bench, unsure what to even do with it now that we're here. The door slowly shuts by itself, trapping us inside. I hear Natalie knocking on the door across the hall, the sound muffled by the closed door and the loud music and, um...

"Let's sit?" I say, plopping down on the bench before I even finish saying those words.

Hannah stares at me, nose scrunched up, her nose ring doing this cute little scrunchy-shifty thing, too.

"Look, um, no offense, I know this is kind of, you know... a night of exploring new things, but I'm not really into girls?" she says.

"Umm?" I murmur, confused. And then. "Oh! Gosh. Um, no. I... I saw you and Oliver and... d-do you want to talk?"

"About Oliver?" Hannah asks, tilting her head to the side, nose still very much scrunched.

"Yes?"

"Ugh! Yes! Please!" Hannah practically screams before tossing herself onto the bench with me. "Charlotte! The ride over was *awful!* I don't even know what's going on. I tried, you know? Like, um... actually, it was me, too. It's my fault? But I don't think he's even into me now? I thought, like... I don't know *what* I thought, but when I saw him outside the library and he said we were supposed to share a ride, I was excited at first? Except that was the most he even talked to me the whole time."

"Wait, really?" I ask. "Ummm... are you sure?"

I mean, I don't know for sure, but I thought Oliver was going to flirt with her in the car at the very least because, you know... I sort of talked about this with him?

Not the car ride. I didn't know about that part. B-but, um... the amateur night dancing part? Yes.

"...To be fair I *did* ask him if he went to stripclubs often..." Hannah reluctantly admits. "Kinda awkward after that."

Something's going on across the hall and I'm not entirely sure what because I can't hear everything over the music. It's not loud enough to block out me talking with Hannah, but with the door shut it's loud enough to block out what's happening outside? I guess this would be useful in most usual circumstances of being in a private room with, you know, a stripper? Because you probably don't want to hear people outside in that case?

I don't actually know, but it makes sense in my head.

"Um, hold on a s-second..." I murmur, opening a door an inch and peeking through.

I have no idea what I'm looking at right now but it's Bella, Angela, and Teddy in a private room together, Bella looking infinitely amused at the situation unfurling in front of her, while Natalie tries to explain to Angela that it's a serious breach of the cheerleader code of conduct to attend a stripclub without informing her first. Angela tries to defend herself while Teddy awkwardly sits on the bench. His eyes meet mine and he waves and, um...

I mouth the word "Sorry" because I think I should be helping him but also I promised Angela I'd keep her secret and I don't even know what's going on anymore so--

I'm sorry, Teddy!

...I'll talk to Angela after?

I quickly shut the door and turn to Hannah and the matter at hand.

"What, um... what did Oliver say after that?" I ask, hoping we can fix whatever the issue is.

"After I asked him if he came to stripclubs often?" Hannah counters, baffled. Then, sarcastic, she says, "He said, oh, yeah, all the time. Strippers love me."

"...I don't think that's true, though?" I point out.

"Me either. I think he was being sarcastic but also I'm so dumb. Why did I say that?!"

"Alright, what happened next?" I ask, still very much hopeful.

We can do this, Hannah! I'll help you! Ummm...

167

WHAT'S A LAP DANCE BETWEEN FRIENDS?

Episode 167

CHARLOTTE

I'm positive we can fix this! Maybe. I don't actually know. But I promised Hannah I'd help her with Oliver. And, um... I also kind of told Oliver I'd help him with Hannah?

I feel like this should be really easy because clearly they both like each other and want to get to know each other better but for some reason it's a whole lot harder than I expected.

Anyways, after Hannah asked Oliver on the ride over if he comes to stripclubs often--

Hannah and I are sitting on a bench in one of the private rooms that are supposed to be for lap dances, but right now we're using it for girl talk. The bench is actually really comfortable, too.

"I told him I was dancing tonight and he said he knows. He, um... he said maybe he'd hang out by the stage when I was on, but, like, no promises. Then I asked him if he..." Hannah hesitates, staring off into the distance like she's reliving an especially embarrassing moment of flirtatious trauma. "Charlotte, I asked him if he liked lap dances..."

"That's, um..." I mumble, because even I know that's probably not a great question to ask. "Huh..."

"I know, right! Like, I went into tonight thinking I'd play it super smooth and start with some lowkey flirting and then ramp it up to a million by the end and toss the dice, pray for a natural twenty, and *bam!* But instead I rolled a one."

"...I don't actually remember what any of that means," I tell her.

"Oh, um... if you roll a twenty on a twenty-sided die for *Caverns & Dragons,* it means you automatically succeed in whatever you're attempting, and in the best way ever. Like, you totally own it, you know?"

"Got it," I say with a nod. "And... a one means?"

"If you roll a one, it's the opposite. You fail no matter what. And, um... not only do you fail, but usually it's in the most gloriously awful way ever. Like, the worst possible fail a person could fail. Which is what I did tonight. I failed so bad, Charlotte. There's no coming back from this. Do you think I should just leave?"

"...Do you want to leave?" I ask.

"Yeah, kinda?" she says, staring at the floor. "I feel pretty dumb, to be honest."

"I feel pretty dumb a lot of the time, but, um... sometimes it's still fine?" I tell her. "Like... you *can* go home. If you really want to. It's okay and no one will be mad. But Jenny and I are here and Teddy's here too and if you want to stay you don't have to flirt with Oliver anymore and dancing will still be fun, right? Oh, we have names, too! You need a name. Um, a stripper name? I'm Chantel. Angela is Bastet b-because, um... cats?"

"Oh my gosh, that's so cool!" Hannah says, giddy. "The Egyptian goddess, right? That's an *amazing* stripper name! Wow. No offense, but I kind of always thought the cheerleaders were a little, um... not dumb, but, you know? Right. Anyways, Bastet! I love it."

"Clarissa's Desire and Jenny went with Cherry Delight," I add, giggling. "So, um... we wanted to be one of each kind of stripper? It's a thing, I guess. You can be a Girl Next Door but that's boring apparently? So hopefully you want to be a Gemstone instead?"

"I'm in," Hannah says, excited now. "I'm definitely in! Like, what kind of Gemstone, though? I love making characters in *Caverns & Dragons* and coming up with names is always the best part, so..."

"There's already a Ruby," I tell her. "And a Crystal. Um... I don't remember the others. Sorry..."

"No, it's fine," Hannah says, determined. "I know what name I want. It's not a full on Gemstone name, but it kind of fits? I think it works."

"We can ask Bella if it's alright," I say, nodding along. "I'm sure it's fine, though."

"*Roxy*," Hannah says, a single sage nod pushing her chin up and then down again. "Tonight I'll be known as... Roxy!"

It's, um... it's not Jade or Amber or Sapphire, which I think are also Gemstone stripper names, but... gems are rocks?

Also Roxy sounds super cute!

"I love it!" I say, excited. "Um, hold on a second?"

"Sure?" Hannah says, confused.

I hop up off the bench and scramble out the door into the hall, nervously knocking on the door I hope Bella's still behind with, um... you know, Teddy and Angela?

The door opens and the platinum blonde bombshell glares out at me, immediately starting to say, "Give me a break. I'm not even on stage for another--"

It's me, though. Not the man behind the counter? Also oh my gosh she's going up on stage before amateur night starts? I want to see! She's so good. I loved watching her dance when Saskia asked her to at Busty Coquette and, um... that was just a quick fun silly thing, but if she dances for real here and now? Oh gosh. *Yes.* I bet it'll be amazing. I can't miss it. I just can't.

"Oh, Chantel," Bella says, giggling, somehow sounding ultra sultry and smooth again. "Everything alright?"

"Um, is Roxy alright as a Gemstone name?" I ask.

"Roxy?" she says, mulling it over, swishing the name across her tongue like a mature red wine. "Yes. It's slightly unorthodox, but I like it. Who's Roxy?"

Hannah's standing in the doorway of our private room. She waves, sheepish, staring with abject awe at the stupidly beautiful stripper in front of her.

"Hi, um, me," Hannah murmurs.

"Nice to meet you, Roxy," Bella says, grinning. "Let's talk soon. I'm trying to teach these two a few tricks while I have the time. Love the nose ring, by the way."

"Thanks!" Hannah says, toying with the smooth circle tucked tightly between either nostril.

Oh, right, I almost forgot...

"Um, is Teddy alright, by the way?" I ask, unsure if it's acceptable to... you know, peek inside the private room?

"Oh, he's *more* than alright..." Bella purrs. "Want to say hi?"

"Sure?"

Bella opens the door a little more and...

Teddy's sitting next to Angela on the bench and she's explaining how, like, you know--

"Lap dances are actually, like, totally a great way to show just how good a friend you are, right?" Angela says, almost sounding like she knows what she's talking about. "Because, like, if you can't give your friend a lap dance, who *can* you give a lap dance to, you know? It's, like, totally a thing, Teddy. So, um... listen, I'm only asking you this because we're friends and I trust you, but, like, is it alright if I practice on you?"

"I just don't think it's a great idea?" Teddy says. "Jenny's *right* outside?"

"Right, *but*," Angela counters. "Jenny thinks you're with *Bella*, so..."

"Technically you *are* with me," Bella points out, glancing over her shoulder at them.

"Uh... this isn't what it looks like, Baby Chantel..." Teddy says, finally realizing I'm standing right there.

"Baby?" Bella asks, lifting one perfect eyebrow.

"I, um... I already know?" I tell him. "It's okay. I won't tell anyone."

"You *told* her?" Teddy gasps, staring hard at Angela. "Angela!"

"Teddy, I'm *Bastet* tonight!" she counters. "Also, look, I mean, how could I *not* tell Charlie? She's totally my BFF and she's the only one I *could* tell. I didn't tell anyone else, I swear! It's still a secret, alright? Like, um... please can we just *try* the lap dance thing?"

"I really don't think friends give friends lap dances, though," Teddy says, stubborn. "That's not even a thing."

"But what if it *were* a thing?" Angela counters. "What then?"

"Uh, it's not, though?"

"Might be awhile," Bella says, winking at me. "See you out there, Chantel?"

I nod and Bella smiles before shutting the door and going back to business. Which is, um...

"Alright, you two," I hear her say. "No more arguing. Here's how this is going to work. Bastet needs to work on her moves for amateur night. Right? And Teddy, you're her friend, correct? I'm going to show her some tricks to try on stage, using you as our practice model. It's purely professional, but also because you're cute and I know you won't get too handsy. I like men like you, Teddy. You know what boundaries are. I'm sure Bastet feels the same. Now, Bastet, after I show you something, you repeat it. Got it?

Afterwards, Teddy tells you what he thinks and you try again. Are we all understood?"

"Yes, ma'am!" Angela readily agrees.

"I mean, if it's for the competition why didn't you just say that in the first place?" Teddy huffs. "Obviously I'll help if that's the case."

"Wait, really?!" Angela asks, excited. "Yay! Thank you, Teddy! And, like, I totally appreciate it. Like, um, I appreciate it so much I'll totally take you into a private room later all by ourselves and show you how much I appreciate it, you know? If, like... you know... if you want to?"

"Uh, sure?" Teddy answers, but he does not, in fact, sound sure.

...I think I should leave them alone now...

"What's going on over there?" Hannah asks, coming into the hallway with me now that we're done with our private room.

"I don't really know?" I answer, truthful.

Hannah shrugs. I shrug. And then we head back to sit with our friends in the showroom, which, um...

HUNTER

"Dude," Olly says to me as soon as we're alone. "I think I fucked up."

I don't know if we're actually alone, though. I mean, philosophical question time or whatever, but can you ever truly be alone when you're in a stripclub? I feel like the answer is no, because if for some reason you *are* sitting alone, that's prime time for a stripper to come over and do a vibe check to see if you're interested in her services as a high-quality naked dance professional, you know?

Which, uh... is exactly what I've been witnessing at the Paper Slipper for the past thirty minutes. It's weird as hell. Like, as a dude, I'm used to, you know... this *not* happening, right? Girls don't generally approach guys, especially when they're wearing the kind of outfits these girls are. You go to a club and see a girl wearing barely anything and dancing her ass off and even if you're the most attractive motherfucker in that place, you're the one doing the approaching.

Here, though? It's a different world entirely. I feel like I somehow got transported to a universe that shouldn't exist and it's trippy as hell, man.

Anyways, Olly and I are chatting and so far a stripper hasn't approached us to see if we want a dance so we're about as alone as two bros can be in a stripclub is what I'm saying.

"Could you please explain the exact moment when you realized you fucked up, though?" I ask, just so I can clarify that quick.

"That's the thing," Olly says, shrugging, absolutely baffled. "I don't even know?"

"Uh, dude, no offense but how can you not know when you fucked up?"

"I think this is a case of somehow having fucked up at a previous point in time when I didn't realize I was fucking up, but I was, in fact, fucking up," Olly says, as if this helps.

"Are you saying this is somehow related to time travel?" I ask, vaguely hopeful.

"No. Dude, what the hell? What does any of this have to do with time travel?"

"I don't know but it kind of sounded like time travel and you got my hopes up."

"Fuck. No. I wish! That'd make everything easier. I could fix it then, you know? Like, go back in time and... fuck you, Jacksy. Nevermind. Don't even get me started. Anyways, the thing is, I thought things were going alright, I was just sitting in the backseat of the Uber with Hannah. I thought I'd keep my mouth shut and say as little as possible because when I talk too much that's usually when I end up saying something stupid, right? And then..."

He pauses for effect but it's not exactly helping because we're in a stripclub and it's easy to get distracted. At the moment, there's this stripper named Cinnamon chatting up the romance book club girls because apparently she's super into books and loves the idea of them coming here for a book club meeting. Chloe is trying to convince Amelia to sit next to the stage of this faux cute and innocent stripper dressed in wedding white named Chastity. Sam's pulling out some dollar bills for her, too.

Jenny and Clarissa are tossing ones at Ruby, who's showing them a few pole dancing moves while this old dude with a massive fucking grin on his face watches from the other side, doing the same. For every dollar the girls add to the pot, the old guy adds two, and he looks more than glad to do it.

Basically what I'm saying is if Olly doesn't get to the point quick, he's going to lose me. I may well already be lost at this point, at least until Baby Sis gets back and distracts me in an entirely different way.

Olly shouts over the music that's banging through the club, mainly because I didn't listen to him the first couple of times and not because the music's too loud.

"She asked me if I come to stripclubs often!" Olly yells. "If that isn't the harshest rejection ever, I don't know what is, man."

"To be fair," I finally answer after scanning the showroom. "You occasionally act like the kind of dude that goes to stripclubs often?"

"Old and rich?" Olly says with a shrug. "I mean, I guess I'll take it."

"That's... not what I meant but if it helps your ego, let's go with it," I say, smirking. "Is that it, though? That doesn't sound like you fucked up too bad?"

"Nah," he says, shaking his head. "After that, like... I told her I come all the time, by the way. Strippers love me. I didn't know what else to say. I figured sarcasm was the way to go. So anyways, we're riding in silence again and I'm trying to figure out what my next move is to, you know, let her know I'm interested but not *too* interested, right? Except then she asks me if I like lap dances."

"She asked you if you like lap dances?" I repeat, because, uh... what? "Dude, that sounds good."

"You'd think so, right? Except instead of asking me in a flirty way, like, you know, insinuating she'd be the one giving me one... nah, the opposite. She did this kind of sneer thing and her nose scrunched up, which, alright, with her nose ring I was pretty into it but she definitely looked at me like I was the scum of the earth, I swear to God."

"Listen," I say, holding back what I really think, which is that Olly definitely fucked up. He already knows that, though. No reason to rub it in. But if he somehow *didn't* fuck up? "Maybe it was dark in the back of the Uber and she wasn't sneering, but she was, like... *smirking* at you? Like a hot and feisty sexy smirk, right? She totally wants to give you a lap dance, buddy."

"I'd be willing to buy that except afterwards she quickly added that she definitely wasn't giving me a lap dance so don't get any ideas."

"Is this a double negative thing, though?" I ask. "That shit always screws with me in English classes."

"Wait, you think so?"

"I'm not saying it is, but... *maybe?*" I offer. "If she definitely *wasn't* giving you a lap dance so *don't* get any ideas, do those two negatives cancel each other out? That's the question we have to ask ourselves, my friend."

"So... alright, for the sake of discussion, if they *do* cancel each other out, where's that leave me?" he asks, brow seriously furrowed, deep in grammatical thought. "She's definitely giving me a lap dance so I better get ideas?"

"I think that's close enough but I'd lean more towards she's definitely giving you a lap dance so get ideas. Adding 'better' to the sentence makes it seem like she's more interested than she might be, you know?"

"Makes sense," Olly says with a nod. "I'm not sure that's what she meant, but I agree with toning it down and tempering my expectations. The lap dance may be happening and I can get ideas about it, but the ideas don't necessarily have to be intense or exaggerated. This may be a case of a casual, friendly lap dance between friends."

"Exactly," I say, nodding back. "Not that that's even a thing, but if it were..."

"Seriously, Jacksy. I fucked up. I don't know what I did. She thinks I'm scum, though. I brought this on myself, didn't I?"

"Probably," I tell him. "Better you find out now than never find out at all though, right?"

"That doesn't make me feel better, but thanks."

"I mean, you're in a club full of hot, half-naked women, so I'm sure you'll be fine, bud," I say, slapping him on the shoulder.

"I don't want to ruin this for you because I appreciate the support, but I don't really want to get a mindless, impersonal lap dance from a random hot stripper. I was kind of hoping for a connection with the nerdy gamer girl with the hottest ass I've ever seen, which may have also included a lap dance, but that continued on into a semi-committed relationship afterwards."

"Isn't that what we all want, Olly?" I say, trying to cheer him up. "I mean, I don't. I have Baby Sis. Who, uh... she'll be dancing and I'll probably get a lap dance later, either here or in private, so--"

"Fucking asshole," Olly grunts, rolling his eyes. "I hate you. I'm going to hang out with Jenny and Clarissa. Maybe I can beg Jenny to forget about the dare so I don't bruise my ego even more."

I smirk, trying not to laugh. "Not gonna happen, but nice dream."

Before Olly heads off to plead his case with Jenny, Teddy slides into the booth with us, hair tousled, looking slightly frazzled.

"Guys," he says. "Hey, uh... hi."

"What's up, bro?" I ask.

"What happened to your hair?" Olly asks.

"Huh? What?" Teddy says, as if he didn't realize the state his hair's in. "Uh, nothing? Look, I don't want to be that guy, but I just, uh... quick question, alright? If a girl says she needs help with something, and you're friends with her, and the help is that she needs to practice her moves because she's entering the amateur night competition at a stripclub, it's not a big deal if she gives you a casual, friendly lap dance, right? Not that this happened to me. I'm, you know... I'm asking for a friend..."

Olly stares at him. I don't even bother. I just sit there and shake my head and sigh. Teddy looks hopeful that we'll somehow believe he's actually asking for a friend, which he's not. You really fucking aren't, Teddy.

"Teddy, go fuck yourself," Olly says, promptly excusing himself from the booth and strolling across the club to see what Jenny and Clarissa and Ruby and the old man over there are up to.

"Shit, did I say something wrong?" Teddy asks, worried.

"Nah, don't worry about it, bud," I say. "It's nothing. How was it, by the way? Your lap dance with Angela?"

Teddy blinks fast, eyes darting this way and that, shifty. It's just us, though. After he realizes this, he calms down a little.

"Dude, she's like... I don't want to say she's into me, because we're just friends, right? But if I didn't know we were just friends, I'd totally say she was into me. I guess that's good, though? It means her lap dance skills are on point, right? I'm kind of jealous. Like, in a friendly way. Whatever guy she's interested in is going to be a really lucky man, Jacksy. Seriously."

...I don't even have the heart to tell him.

Teddy will figure it out on his own.

Some day.

Maybe.

Probably not.

CHARLOTTE

Hannah and I are heading back to the showroom so we can hang out with everyone for a little while before the amateur night competition officially starts when, um...

One second I'm walking side by side with Hannah, the next second she's slightly in front of me and nervously heading over to hang out with Jenny, Clarissa, and Olly, who are sitting around a stage watching Ruby perform some really good pole maneuvers, then, um...

The next thing I know I'm pulled into a dark corner behind a pillar that's covered in the same plush red carpet as the stripclub floor.

"Sit!" a girl demands, basically pushing me onto a bouncy leather bench seat.

I squeak and flop onto it and I definitely bounce and my robe almost comes undone so I flail and grab at the ends and pull it close to my chest, hiding my, um... I don't know if it's a naughty secret because I'm in a stripclub and there's a lot of girls wearing a whole lot less than me, but despite all that I feel like I need to stay covered right now.

"Um, hi, what?" I say as soon as I realize who pulled me to the side.

"Don't say *hi* to me," Erica snaps. "Who do you think you are? Is it Chantel or is it Charlotte?"

"I... um... b-both?" I answer. "Bella and Ruby said I needed to have a... a stripper name for tonight? For the competition? So, um... my real name is still Charlotte, but, um... my stripper name is Chantel? You can have a stripper name, too!" I add, just in case she doesn't realize and wants one?

I feel like I should've asked her earlier. Maybe Erica feels left out. I know how that feels and I wouldn't want to make her feel the same, even if she's been really mean to me in the past.

"You think I'm dumb, is that it?" she counters, staring hard. "I'm not an idiot, Chantelotte! Ha! That sounds awful but you deserve it. Anyways, I'm not trying to be friends with you if that's what you think. I have my stripper name picked out. Clearly I'm the best girl here, so I'm going with Lusty Diamond. I wrote it down on the form already."

"Oh," I say, nodding. "I, um... I need to fill that out still."

I should actually do that now. We only have fifteen minutes before the competition starts.

"Right, which is why I pulled you aside," Erica says, sneering. "I didn't want to do it like this, especially since you seem to have some naive idea that you can somehow beat me fair and square, but, well... you haven't actually looked at what it takes to enter the competition, have you?"

"...No?" I answer. It's... a form and you fill it out and I'm pretty sure that's it?

Erica slaps the form down on the small circular table in front of me, all filled out and ready to go. Instead of pointing to any of that, she taps her long-nailed finger on a box at the bottom which says:

"Amateur Night Entry Fee: $50"

I stare at it for far longer than I want to admit because, um... b-because...

"Do you even have that much?" she asks with a nasty smirk. "I doubt it. Just between you and me, we both know you couldn't have even afforded your stupid little laptop if Lance hadn't given you his employee discount, and that wasn't even that long ago, so..."

"I, um... I don't... b-but--!" I start to say, because the competition starts in less than fifteen minutes now and there's no way I can get fifty dollars before then.

"Exactly," Erica scoffs. "If you can't pay, you can't enter, and you lose by default. I win and that's that. I mean, look, I'll still dance because that's what I came here to do, but since you lose and I'm the winner, I'm going to go claim my new sexy stepbro and show him exactly what kind of stepsister I can be for him, on the stage, in a private room out back, and later I'm going to take him back to his mom's place, because I just so happen to know it's not too far away and she's away on a business trip right now and..."

She says the next words very very slowly and with heavily exaggerated pronunciation.

"*All. Night. Long.*"

"I... I don't think H-Hunter will--" I start to say.

"Do you think I *care* what you think?" she snaps. "Look, you fool, you lost, fair and square. This is it. You're finished. Now don't be a sore loser and just give me what's mine and go away. Shoo shoo, Charlotte! You aren't even a stripper now. You can dress up all you want but you're a fake. You--"

Someone steps out from behind the plush red carpet-covered pillar while Erica's ranting. The newcomer stands there quietly, hands folded in front of her, waiting for Erica to finish or to acknowledge her or, um... I don't actually know but she's very calm and professional and she's wearing the usual black pencil skirt and crisp white blouse she always wears.

Natalie pushes her glasses up her nose and clears her throat as soon as Erica inadvertently glances at her.

"What do *you* want?" Erica pounces. "Go away!"

"Gladly," Natalie says, prim and proper. "I didn't mean to interrupt. I just wanted to give this to Chantel. She dropped it after I gave it to her in our private room earlier."

"She... what?" Erica asks, confused.

"The lap dance was *excellent,* by the way," Natalie says, winking at me.

...I know I didn't give Natalie a lap dance and we weren't in a private room together but she hands me a fifty dollar bill which is exactly what I need right now, so...

I stare at the money in my hand and Erica does the same and before I can say anything Natalie walks off without another word.

"I, um... I can enter the competition now?" I say. "Yay..."

Erica seethes. Her entire face turns red, angry and hot. It's not like my cheeks when I'm embarrassed and blushing, either. This is a very very grim and angry and upset color of red, the likes of which I could never match, not in a million years. I just don't think I could ever be that angry about something but I don't know yet because maybe I can and I haven't found the thing I could get that angry about? Ummm...

"*This isn't over!*" Erica screeches. "*I'm going to destroy you and ruin your life and steal Hunter back because he's mine!*"

She storms off without another word, except, um...

"W-wait!" I call after her.

"*What!*" she howls. It's, um... that's another word...

"You f-forgot your submission form...?" I murmur, nervously picking it up and holding it out for her.

Erica wails at me but it's more of a very loud high-pitched sound, no words necessary. She snatches the form out of my hands, attempts to stomp off very loudly except the carpet under her feet muffles the sound, making it all but impossible. She tries to stomp even louder but it's really not working and I, um... I don't know what to say but she seems incredibly irate at the fact that she can't stomp loud enough?

...Uh huh...

Right, so...

Bella slinks into the bouncy leather bench next to me, wrapping her slender arm around my shoulder, her long platinum blonde hair mixing with mine as she leans in close, the sides of our heads touching, intimate and close.

"Good job," she says, kissing my cheek. "Now go find your man, fill out the form, and get ready to dance your sexy little ass off, alright?"

I blush and kiss her cheek back because I don't know if that's what I'm supposed to do but, um... she looks at me, surprised, and laughs.

"Okay," I say, excited. "Um, thank you for helping me..."

...I don't mention that I'm not sure my butt is sexy enough to dance it off, but I'll try my best...

"Anytime, honey," Bella says, smiling gently. Her smile turns into a grin a second later. "Don't thank me yet, though. Just wait until you see the shoes I have in store for you later..."

I forgot about that part.

I've, um... I've been wearing my old sneakers this entire time?

I hurry away to rejoin Hunter who is sitting with Teddy and, um... oh, Angela's there now, too.

I won't tell anyone, Teddy! Or Angela. I promise.

Can I tell Hunter soon, though?

OFF LIMITS ALLURE

Episode 168

CHARLOTTE

I scramble to finish filling out the amateur night entry form before the final deadline which is in, um...

Five minutes?

All the other girls finished theirs already, handed them in, and paid the entry fee. Which, um... I guess we get to keep our tips, if we even get tips, which I have no idea how tips work but this is apparently a thing and I'm going to get tips so maybe it's fine. I need to pay Natalie back, though. I know she made it seem like I left fifty dollars behind but I definitely didn't so, um...

Alright, so, yes!

The problem is that there's a lot going on in the stripclub right now and it's sort of distracting. It's not like the entry form is all that complicated, you know?

Name? That's, um... this shouldn't actually be hard to answer but I don't know if I'm supposed to use my real name or my fake ID name and so I leave it blank for now.

Stage name? Chantel. Easy. This one is easy.

Date of Birth? This should also be easy, but, um... for the same reason that my name is hard, this is also hard...

Height? Weight? Eye color? Hair color? I don't really know why those are important but I fill them in as best I can.

And finally...

Choose Your Song:

This is the song I'll be dancing to on stage and according to the form I can pick basically anything as long as it's readily accessible on a standard music streaming platform so...

I write my choice down because I have no hesitation whatsoever about it. I've been using our free time during pole dancing classes to practice some of my moves for tonight and I haven't actually been able to do the full choreography for reasons that will become evident during my time on stage, but... I feel pretty confident?

About the routine. That's really it. I don't feel confident about anything else. I don't know if anyone's even going to like it, but *I* like it, and this is just for fun, and that's what's important, and--

I scribble what I remember of the name of the song and the person who sings it next to the question on the form and then I go back to figure out the rest.

Hunter and the boys are sitting at a different table, giving me some space, when suddenly...

"One minute to go before we kick off the event you've all been waiting for!" the DJ roars through the microphone in his booth in the back of the club. "We have a ton of girls to introduce you to tonight. I know you're going to love each and every one of them. I mean, look at 'em, fellas? And the best part? They're all brand spanking new to the scene! Spanking not included, unless you're lucky and one of these sexy ladies gives you permission. We don't want to have to kick anyone out before the fun starts, now do we?"

Oh gosh oh gosh oh gosh what do I--

Ruby slides into the booth with me, smiling quietly while I try to figure out what to write next.

"Need help?" she asks.

"I... m-maybe?" I answer.

"Fake ID, huh?" Ruby says without me even mentioning it.

Probably the fact that I don't know my own name or date of birth is a good indicator...

"...Please don't tell anyone?" I mumble.

"I mean, you're eighteen so it's fine, Chantel," Ruby says, giggling. "Bruno's a different story, though. He might get mad if he finds out. So I'd put down whichever name you came in on. And, you know, hurry it up! Less than a minute to go, girl."

I jot down my fake name and, um... I have to check the ID for my fake date of birth but I scribble that down fast, too. Instead of handing it in on my own, Ruby snatches the form away as soon as I'm done, along with the fifty dollar bill I left sitting on the table. She bounces up, flashes me a silly smile with a big wink, and then sashays over to give my form to the floor manager.

"The countdown begins!" the DJ says. "Amateur Night officially starts in... five... four... three... two... and--"

Ruby pretends to slow down as if she's going to miss the deadline but the floor manager already sees her with a form in hand. He rolls his eyes at her and she turns back, waving to me. I giggle and I'm excited and--

The announcement comes through right as she slips the sheet of paper into the grumpy man's hand.

"GENTLEMAN, LET THE GAMES BEGIN!"

There's, um... there's a little more to it than that but this is how it starts...

HUNTER

"Guys," I say to the guys as we sit in our own booth,

letting the girls do their thing. "What the fuck is going on over there?"

Mainly even though the girls we know are competing are already dressed up and ready to go, there's a short break before the contest officially begins. Apparently Bella's leading the charge, shepherding the amateurs. She took the girls into the bathroom so they could change, finish getting ready, do whatever, who even knows with girls? They're always going into some bathroom somewhere for one reason or another, you know?

Anyways, my previous point stands: *What the fuck is going on over there?*

"Do you think we should invite him to sit with us?" Teddy asks, moderately clueless.

I don't even know how he can be like this right now. Teddy, we're in a goddamn stripclub. Stop being so fucking wholesome, dude. You literally spent twenty minutes in a private room getting lap dances from Angela and a professional stripper. I don't understand.

"I'm kind of on the fence about it, but maybe?" Olly says with a shrug. "On the one hand, watching what's going on is really entertaining. On the other hand, if we invite him to sit with us, maybe the girls will join, too?"

"I don't want to ruin this for you, boys," Sam says with a reluctant sigh. "But I think we're off limits tonight."

"Why?" I ask, being an asshole for the hell of it. "I mean, I get why I'm off limits. I kind of even get why Teddy's off limits. You, though? No real reason you should be. No clue about Olly, either. He's totally not off limits. Literally none of the girls have staked a claim over him whatsoever."

"I don't even know what we're talking about," Teddy points out. "Off limits for what?"

"Dude," all of us say, staring hard at him.

"Can we just talk normally for once?" Teddy asks. "I don't

know why everything has to be such a big secret! Come on, guys."

"Fair enough, Teddy," Olly says, nodding, super serious for, like... two seconds and that's it. "I think what Jacksy's referring to is the fact that for some reason Lance over there has about three strippers begging for his dick. And, you know, we don't have any?"

"I think they're just being nice and helping him study?" Teddy says with a shrug. "He's clearly studying. He brought his textbooks and everything."

...This is technically true and I vaguely remember Lance mentioning he had to study tonight but I didn't think he'd actually do it, you know?

Like, come on, dude, you're in a stripclub.

To be fair, the romance book club girls were reading a romance novella earlier too, though. Some of the strippers loved that, so who knows?

Do they really love it? Is this all just a part of their game? Are they only in it for the money?

I have no idea. I feel like it's impolite to ask a stripper that, and also if you asked one they'd probably lie their ass off because no one wants to hear someone's only interested in you for your money, you know? I mean, it's probably true, but still.

"Can we talk about Teddy for a second, though?" Sam adds, in case we forgot.

"What'd I do now?" Teddy asks, confused.

"Your excursion into a private room to get a lap dance from not only the hottest stripper in the club, but the fact that you were there with Angela at the same time, who's subjectively the hottest girl at our school?" I offer.

"*Guys,*" Teddy huffs. "I *told* you. It's not like that. Bella was just being nice. Nothing happened. And Angela needed help with her dance routine. That's it."

"So you had two stupidly hot blondes grinding on your

lap and you're saying, what, you *didn't* get a raging hard-on?" Olly asks.

Teddy fidgets side to side, refusing to answer.

"Thought so. Fuck you, Teddy."

"Guys, let's not pile on Teddy," I tell them. "But seriously, what do we do about Lance?"

"Nothing?" Sam says. "He looks fine?"

"I'm just saying, it's not his fault he's Erica's stepbrother, you know?"

"I do feel kind of bad for the dude," Olly adds. "Not a lot, just a little bit."

"If you guys want to invite him over, that's fine, but despite the fact that he's got three sets of tits shoved in his face I think the man is actually studying," Sam points out. "So..."

"Okay, I'll do it," I say. "If he wants to join us, let's be nice. He gave Baby Sis a discount on her laptop, so he's not a bad guy."

"He seems cool," Teddy says, nodding. "I mean, I don't know him that well, but every time we see him he seems cool?"

"You're way too nice, Teddy," I say. "But in a good way, you know? Love you, dude."

"Aw, thanks, Jacksy! Love you too, man."

And so... you know, I slip away from the guys for a second to talk to Lance who's surrounded by three stupidly attractive strippers; Gia, the Latina one from earlier, Angel, the pale skinned dark-haired girl with white wedding-style lingerie, and this other one named Lexi who Bella says has a dumb name and she's kind of tomboyish and slender instead of curvy but somehow it works.

"Hey, uh... Lance?" I say, really fucking unsure how to interrupt the dude when he's surrounded by three half-naked strippers.

"Is this your friend?" Lexi asks, tilting her head to the side, staring me up and down. "He's cute."

"He's off limits," Gia says, pretending to sound sad about it, pouting it up and everything. "Bella's girl's boy."

"Bella's not here and neither is her girl, though..." Angel adds, mischievous and seductive. "*Hmmmm...*"

"Uh, hey, hi Hunter," Lance says, unsure how to respond while, you know, surrounded by three strippers. "What's going on, man?"

"You look busy, so feel free to stay here if you want, but if you want to join us over there, it's cool, you know?" I say. "The guys and I just wanted to invite you over if you wanted, that's all."

"Awwww, are you leaving us already, Lance?" Lexi says, curling close, holding his arm, basically clinging to him.

"Weren't you going to do that Pomodoro technique thing, honey?" Gia adds. "Study for twenty-five minutes while we take care of all your needs, and then go to a private room for a five minute lap dance break?"

Holy fucking shit, why have I never thought of that? That's the best goddamn studying technique in the fucking world. Who the hell knew? Having a serious talk with Baby Sis about that one later, for sure.

"I know we said we'd take turns, but two is better than one, right?" Angel purrs, anything but angelic.

"I just want him all to myself, though!" Lexi says, pouty. "But... I guess I can share if I have to..."

"Right," I say, because seriously I don't know how to have this conversation. Good luck, Lance. I believe in you. "The offer's there if--"

I start to leave, to let the strippers do their thing, but suddenly Lance shoots up, politely wrestles his arm out from between Lexi's nearly non-existent but still somehow surprisingly enticing boobs, and, you know...

"Wait up!" he says, grabbing his textbooks off the table and hurrying to follow after me. "Uh, sorry, ladies! I mean, you're all really nice and maybe I can, uh, after? I need to finish studying first."

"Oh no! He's leaving us!" Gia says, letting out the deepest sigh, her tits jiggling way more than I ever thought humanly possible.

Lance stares. I don't blame him. It's like a black hole, except bouncy and curvy, just sucking you in no matter what. The only reason I've managed to resist is I didn't look in the first place. I only accidentally spotted the jiggle out of the corner of my eye and then immediately turned to thoughts of Baby Sis and what it's going to be like watching her dance on a pole in a few minutes or, you know, whenever it's her turn to pole dance.

"No fair," Lexi says, hands on her hips, glaring at Gia's wobbling assets.

"Stop making Lexi jealous, Gia," Angel says, playing the mediator. "I'm sure there's plenty of gentlemen in the club for each of us. We can fight over Lance when he's done studying and needs a well-deserved break. Which... come find me, baby? I *really* want to take care of you..."

She locks eyes with him and bats her lashes like she's temptation personified. Fuck, dude. You're done for. No joke. Good luck, buddy.

"Yeah, uh... yeah..." Lance says, nearly falling for it, almost dropping everything right then and there to rush to a private room for whatever she has to offer.

I know common knowledge says never fall in love with a stripper but I guess I can see why people do?

Anyways...

Lance follows me without a word until we get back to the guys and then--

"Look, you guys are great," Olly says, pretending to be serious. "But I think I have to study, too. Lance, my man, you have a textbook I can borrow?"

"Uh, I only brought this one?" he says, apologetic. "The other one is Erica's. My final exams are next week and I'm not doing so great in English, you know? I'm acing my math and computer science classes, so that's good, but if I don't pass my English exam I'm going to have to retake it next year and... yeah..."

"Don't listen to Olly," I say, clapping our new friend on the back. "He's just being a dick. Also he's trying to hook up with the nerd girl with the nose ring from earlier, so..."

"That's over, Jacksy," Olly says with a sigh. "Seriously, I tried my best, but..."

"Are you talking about Hannah?" Teddy asks, oblivious. "What happened?"

"I don't even know what happened, but I'm sure it can be summed up by saying Olly was being Olly," Sam says, which, yeah... pretty much? You got it, dude.

"Nah, it's cool, bud," Olly says, shaking his head. "I'm gonna give it one more shot when she's dancing, but if it's not meant to be then it's not meant to be, you know? I'll move on with a heavy heart and a hard dick."

"No truer words have ever been spoken, my friend," Sam says, nodding in agreement.

"I think when you're trying to get a girl you're not supposed to tell her how hard your dick is?" I remind him. "Like, just letting you know in case that was part of your actual strategy."

"Yeah, no, that wasn't part of my plan," Olly says. "I figured I'd console myself by paying for a lap dance if it doesn't work out."

"Seriously, I can talk to her if you want?" Teddy says, always a team player.

Right, so, anyways--

The girls will be back soon. The DJ's getting everything set up for Bella to take over. Apparently she's the event coordinator for tonight and she'll be doing live commentary with some other stripper named Crystal? No idea.

"Is Jacksy's ex going to be mad that you're sitting with us, Lance?" Sam asks.

"No clue," Lance says, annoyed. "She gets mad at the weirdest things, you know? Like, the other day when we were home, she was taking a shower and texted me that she forgot her towel in her room? So I went and left it outside the bathroom door for her and texted her back to let her know and... she was *mad* about it? I don't know what more she wants from me? I did exactly what she asked me to do."

"That *is* really weird," Teddy says, oblivious. "I'd do the same. Jenny just shouts at me from the bathroom, though. I tried opening the door to slip the towel in for her one time and she screamed so loud I thought we were being robbed."

"I know, right!" Lance says, exasperated. "I mean, Erica's never shouted at me for that, but I thought it was the best thing to just leave the towel outside. It's not like anyone else was home."

"Ugh. Sisters are the worst," Teddy groans. "I get it."

"Teddy, she's technically his *step*sister," Olly points out. "Same as Baby Sis is Jacksy's stepsister, you know?"

"I mean, that's different though," Teddy says, still clueless.

"I'm just saying, man. It's not like it would be that bad if Lance walked in on her, right?"

"It could be pretty bad, Olly," Teddy counters. "Have you ever been screamed at by your sister? It's not fun."

"Exactly," Lance says with a nod. "It's awful."

"You guys might have a point," Olly says, trying not to laugh. "I don't have a sister, so..."

"You did get to see Jenny's boobs once, though?" Sam says, looking on the bright side.

"Guys! Seriously, can we *not* talk about that?" Teddy says with a sigh. "I know I said I was fine with it at the time, but I didn't think it'd come up during every other conversation, you know?"

"Dude, I didn't even bring it up this time!" Olly says, defensive. "Sam did. I wasn't going to. I mean, now that he mentions it, it probably would've been better if it happened when she was in the shower, though? Slippery wet tits are definitely more fun to look at than, you know, regular non-wet ones, and in this case--"

Teddy shakes his head, rolls his eyes, and holds his hands over his ears.

"I hate that I find this amusing but we really should be nice to Teddy, guys," I say. "And, look... I get where Lance is coming from, too. If it were any other stepsister? Yeah, maybe. Erica? No fucking way."

"I don't even know why I'm here," Lance adds. "What the hell is a Stepbro Triathlon? The girls are competing, not us."

"That's a *very* valid point," I say with a nod. "Technically it should be the Stepsister Triathlon. Huh."

"Right? Exactly!"

"Hey, not to interrupt, but have you guys seen Chloe and Amelia lately?" Sam says, glancing around the club.

Fuck. They're gone? Uh...

CHARLOTTE

We're supposed to be getting ready before taking our turns dancing on stage, but as soon as we get into the bathroom to change--

Catastrophe strikes!

It has nothing to do with me but I still feel bad?

First off, um... I should point out that it's not just me, Clarissa, Angela, Jenny, Hannah, and Erica competing. There's four more girls and two of them look polished and professional and the other two look like maybe they've done this a couple times but I don't know. I'm too shy to talk to them and they look older and more mature and, um... I mean, not *that* old. Like twenty-five? Or somewhere around that age, but definitely not young college students.

But besides that, as soon as we get into the bathroom, Angela remembers Hannah's here because, you know... Hannah showed up when Angela was in a private room with Teddy.

"*You!*" Angela says, glaring hard at the girl with the nose ring. "I've totally heard *everything* about you and I don't like it! Not one bit!"

"Not even a little bit!" Clarissa adds, playing hype woman to her cheerleader friend. "Wait, what did we hear and why don't we like it?"

"Babe," Angela says, turning to explain. "This is her, remember? The girl who invited Teddy over for a sleepover? Jenny told us about her."

"Aww, that's super cute!" Clarissa squees. "Love it! Good for Teddy."

"Um, that happened years ago and I apologized to Jenny for it already?" Hannah says.

"It's not about what happened *then*, it's about what's totally happening *now!*" Angela counters. "I know what you're up to and I won't let you steal *him* away from me. Totally. You, um... *you...*"

"No bad words," Clarissa reminds her. "Even if we don't like another girl, we need to remember that we shouldn't knock other women down. We need to be supportive and strong, even when we don't want to be."

"*Ugh!*" Angela shrieks. "You're totally right, babe. Sorry. I almost did it, too. Anyways, look, Hannah. Wait, did you pick a stripper name for tonight? What is it?"

"I did!" Hannah says, excited for a second, forgetting what else is going on. "Charlotte told me we were all going with different kinds of names, so I went with a Gemstone one. I know it's kind of different but... Roxy? That's it."

"Whoa," Angela says, eyes wide in appreciation. "Cute. Love it. But look, even if you picked a cute name and you're totally rocking the trendy hipster aesthetic with that nose ring and your hair is, like... I couldn't pull off a hairstyle like that but it looks really hot on you. What I'm trying to say is *he's* mine so..."

"Um, who, though?" I ask, not entirely sure if I should enter the conversation or not.

"I'm curious, too," Jenny adds, coming up beside me. "Who are they fighting over?"

"It's, um... it's n-not..." Oh gosh, it *is* Teddy, isn't it? But Jenny can't find out. "D-definitely not Teddy..." I finish, mumbling.

Angela blinks as if she's only now realizing Jenny's in the same bathroom as us. Which, um... she's been in the same bathroom as us this entire time so I don't quite understand that but I guess it happens?

"Look, I'm not just going to say his name out loud, but you know who I'm talking about," Angela says to Hannah. "I'm Bastet, by the way. Rawr! Kitty power! *Me~ow*."

"I... I don't even think he's interested, so..." Hannah says, sulking. "I came into tonight kind of hopeful, but if he's more interested in you then I doubt I have a chance. Especially not against a cheerleader."

"Babe, don't even say that!" Angela says, rushing over to hug her. "I was, like, totally a little harsh before, but, for real... you're hot and don't let anyone tell you differently. I mean, sometimes being hot isn't enough, though? And that's frustrating, because, like, what if the guy you like wants a girl who is into roller skating or whatever? And you *can't* roller skate and it totally annoys you because you know if you *could* roller skate he'd totally be into you, but..."

"Can't you just learn how to roller skate, though?" Clarissa says, tilting her head to the side. "I don't get it."

"Babe, you can't just *learn* to roller skate, you know?"

Angela says, shaking her head, sad. "It doesn't work like that."

"I mean, it kind of does, though?" Jenny says, confused.

"It might be hard and it could take awhile?" I add, helpful.

"They don't understand," Angela says, looking to Hannah once more. "And, like, that's just how love is, am I right? *We* understand, Roxy. You and me. We totally do. Right? So, like... be strong out there. You deserve to find a man, even if this one is totally mine and I wish he had a twin brother or something except, like, alright, if he *did* have a twin brother, the fantasy of having both would always be there and that's probably way too forbidden but also stupidly hot, so I don't even know, but, like, we could share? Except we can't, because there's no twin brother."

"...I think I understand but you lost me about halfway through the end of that," Hannah says.

"Who are we even talking about, though?" Jenny asks. "What boy? Is he here?"

"Look, he isn't *not* here," Angela says, winking at me. "See what I did there, Chantel?"

"Um, yes?"

It's... a double negative, so...

Also I'm very confused because I thought Angela was talking about Teddy but now I think Hannah's talking about Oliver? In which case Angela can have Teddy and Hannah can have Oliver.

But they aren't twins or brothers at all, so is that the problem now?

"So... he *is* here?" Jenny says, already catching on.

"Shoot, I thought I'd hidden that well," Angela grumbles.

"Can you *amateurs* spend a little more time focusing on the contest and less time with the dumb college girl drama?" one of the definitely professional and not even amateur girls on the other side of the bathroom says, glaring at us.

"It's funny, but also sad," her friend adds. "Which means it'll be even funnier when you lose, so..."

"Alright, that's enough of that," Bella says, taking charge. "If everyone's ready, I'll explain how tonight's going to go. I know *some* of you already know..." She glares at the pros from another stripclub before continuing. "If I had my way, this would only be actual amateurs, but unfortunately it's not my call."

"No idea what you're talking about!" the first pro girl says, giggling, smug.

"Hehehe..." her friend adds, bouncing up and down on her toes.

Bella rolls her eyes. "Right. Now if we could all--"

Before she can finish that thought, one of the bathroom stall doors bursts open, smacking loudly against the outside of the stall right next to it. Erica struts out in stripper heels and some kind of outfit, sashaying to the center of the bathroom before pivoting on her heels, twirling in a half circle, and confronting the rest of us.

"Your *goddess* is *here!*" Erica proclaims, holding her arms out in front of her, hands upraised, ready to accept any and all praise aimed her way.

Which, um... mostly everyone just blinks and stares at her but she seems fine with that, too?

Also... oh gosh... seriously, her outfit is--

It makes everyone else in the bathroom look like they're completely covered and ready for church. A barely there string bikini "covers" her... bottom, sort of... and her top is also "covered" at least as far as her nipples go. The rest...? Not so much. Her outfit also looks like it's going to fall off if she so much as moves the wrong way, let alone dances. And, as if this helps but it definitely doesn't, she's wearing an equally revealing fishnet mesh top with leggings to match. It does absolutely nothing to cover anything, especially since the "net" part is pretty wide and see-through.

Her entire outfit is black? Does that help? Including her very high-heeled stripper shoes that she can somehow walk incredibly well in. She clicks her heels across the tiled bathroom floor, taking an alluring step back to let everyone else bask in her sultry glory.

"There's always one," Bella says. "Look, *goddess*, the way this works is--"

"Lusty Diamond," Erica snaps. "That's my name. Remember it. Thanks. Not that anyone will be able to forget after I step on stage!"

"What's she wearing?" Clarissa asks, tilting her head this way and that, trying to figure it out from different angles.

"I don't know, babe," Angela answers. "But, like, remember, even if it's Erica, we shouldn't say mean things, so..."

CHERRY DELIGHT!

Episode 169

CHARLOTTE

 fter everyone finishes arguing in the stripclub bathroom, Bella explains the rules for amateur night, which are:

- 1.) For the duration of the competition, all entrants must sit together in a special reserved section. You're allowed to cheer on your fellow dancers, but booing is strictly prohibited. No loud talking during another girl's performance, either.

- 2.) When your name is called, get your butt up on stage pronto. You'll be given a minute to introduce yourself and play up whatever fantasy you want. When it comes to men in stripclubs, the fantasy is just as important as how much skin you show, if not even more so. Men can see naked women anywhere nowadays, so give them a reason to want to see *YOU*.

- 3.) The Paper Slipper is a stripclub. Obviously stripping is encouraged. You can remove as many articles of clothing as you want during the duration of your dance, with the exception of your thong, underwear, panties, whatever you're wearing down under as a last line of defense. Those need to stay on. Also, please remember this is a *strip*club, not a *sex*club, meaning implied sexual acts on stage are fine but don't go overboard. *("I'm looking at you, Lusty Diamond. If that thong so much as slips to the side, we're having words.")*

- 4.) The winner of the competition isn't determined solely by tips, but while you're on stage you may have men bidding for your affection. Play it up as much as you want. You keep whatever tips you make during your dance, but you should also be tipping your set DJ after the competition at the very least. More on this later.

- 5.) Once everyone's performed, the winner will be decided by audience approval. This means the louder you can get the crowd to cheer you on, the better chance you have to win. We'll go girl by girl and ask for a round of applause. If in doubt, as a tiebreaker, we'll give the two final girls one last chance to show their moves before doing a last round of applause between the two finalists. The winner takes home the entire thousand dollars.

- 6.) Once the contest is over, you're welcome to stay and "work the club" if you want. You're allowed use of the private rooms, gentlemen may come up and ask you for a dance, and you can even use the VIP room if you want. A percentage of the money you make from private lap dances or VIP room use will be paid out as a tip to Jerry, the man in the back keeping you safe. Tip generously and you'll be treated in kind. Don't be stingy. Word gets around fast.

- 7.) While you can mingle and talk with customers in the club, under no circumstances are you allowed to give lap dances in the main showroom. You also won't be included in the hourly roundup of girls who go up on stage. Your only chance to bring in money tonight is the competition itself and the private rooms afterwards. No exceptions. Trust me, the floor manager has no qualms about kicking you out.

- 8.) Besides that, have fun, enjoy yourself, don't do anything you don't want to do, if you ever feel unsafe then let me or one of the other girls know. We take care of our own. You're one of us tonight. If you need someone to walk you outside once you're done, talk to me or Bruno out front and we'll arrange it.

And, um... I think that's it but I really wish I had a notebook so I could've written that down because it's kind of a lot and...

"Alright, ladies and gentleman!" Bella announces from the DJ booth in front of the club's center stage. There's three stages total, each with a pole, but we're only using the middle one for the contest. "Amateur night's about to begin. We have ten lovely ladies for you to choose from tonight. I'll be calling them up one by one to introduce themselves. If you want to get a closer look, feel free to approach the stage at this point, but if you aren't laying dollar bills out during their dance then get your stingy ass back to your seat. Show them what they're worth, people! And don't forget to stick around afterwards, because if you're lucky you may be able to take one of these beauties into the backroom for a special show if you know what I mean..."

I'm sitting by Angela and Jenny, with Clarissa a little further away. Hannah's sitting with us, too. Erica's kind of off on her own, keeping her distance from the rest of the girls. The two women who Bella claims are professionals from another club are seated by themselves at the far end of our special reserved section, with the last two girls sitting between me and my friends and them.

...I belatedly realize there's a lot more people in the stripclub showroom than I first realized...

It's, um... it's not fully packed, not like a sold out stadium audience or anything, but there's more people sitting in seats than not, most of the tables full up. To be fair, some of the working girls are sitting with the men, too. And then, um... there's Hunter and the boys sitting together, and the romance book club girls sitting at their own table, too. Chloe and Amelia are kind of in between both groups, sitting next to Sam but also right by the book club girls.

I, um... I knew there'd be people here but I didn't realize there'd be so many? I... I need to dance in front of... oh gosh...

...*How...*

HUNTER

"Uh, guys," I say to the boys. "How are we supposed to do this?"

"It's a stripclub," Olly says, being a dick. "I think you're supposed to sit back, relax, and enjoy the show, buddy."

"Dude, I know where we are," I snap back. "I'm saying, like... we need to support the girls, right? So... how are we supposed to do *that?*"

"I think," Sam says, being a fucking smartass. "I mean, at least according to what Bella just said, we approach the stage with money in our hands and make it rain when someone we like is dancing on stage."

"*Dude*," I say again, more insistent this time. "I know that, too! I'm saying, like... *which* girls are we supposed to each individually support and *how* the fuck do you guys want to do *that?*"

"As much as I want to be generally supportive of Jenny, I don't think I can sit next to the stage when she's up," Teddy says, as if this is any real big news. "Sorry, guys."

"It's cool, Teddy," Sam says, patting him on the back. "I'll support her plenty for the both of us, alright?"

"Thanks, Sam," Teddy says with a nod, which, uh... come on, Teddy.

"Look, I'm shooting my shot again and I have a plan, so I'm going up when Hannah's on stage," Olly says, as if none of us knew this, either. "But I'm all for supporting Jenny, too. I mean, it's the least I can do since she showed me her tits during Truth or Dare, right?"

Teddy narrows his eyes at Olly, because half of that's supportive and the other half is being a dick. I get it, Teddy. I don't know what I'd do in that situation, either.

"I'm supporting my roomie, clearly," Chloe says. "Go roomie! Yeah!"

"I mean, obviously I'm also supporting Baby Sis," I say. "But, like... look, I'm not saying I want an up close view of everyone else dancing, but shouldn't we maybe support all the girls? It's the nice thing to do, right?"

"On the one hand, yes," Sam says. "On the other hand, depending on how it goes, I can see at least one of us getting our balls ripped off by the end of the night doing that."

"...Yeah," I grunt, because... yeah...

"What if we just ask the girls what they want?" Teddy offers.

Amelia nervously nods, agreeing with Teddy. I don't think stripclubs are really her thing, which, you know, I get it. No judgement there.

"So, the problem as I see it," I point out. "Teddy's going to do... what? When Jenny comes on, what were you planning, bud?"

"Ruby said I could hang out in a private room with her when Jenny's on," Teddy says. "I guess there's this song she really likes that she wants to show me back there?"

"...Guys, why did we bring Teddy here again?" I ask, sighing. What the fuck, bro?

"Uh, what about me?" Lance adds, looking up from his textbook. "Erica told me to take a break from studying during the competition. I've been getting a lot done so far so it's probably fine."

"I mean, are you supporting her or what?" I ask. "I don't know, dude. Do what makes you happy, I guess?"

"Is it weird if I support her?" he asks. "She's my stepsister, so I feel like I should, but also... I mean, it's weird, right?"

"Jacksy's doing it," Olly says with a shrug.

"He sure is!" Sam says, grinning ear to ear. "What a great stepbrother you are, buddy."

"Shut your fucking pretty boy mouth," I say, rolling my eyes at him. "Anyways, look," I continue, talking to Lance. "Erica's fucking weird, dude. She has some crazy ideas about stepbrothers, you know? So, like... I know this is some wild competition between her and Baby Sis, but don't get dragged into her craziness too much, alright?"

"Is this like that saying?" Olly asks. "Don't stick your dick in crazy?"

"I mean, basically," I say, nodding and in full agreement. "Dude, don't do that, either."

"I wasn't planning on it?" Lance says, absolutely fucking baffled.

I have no idea how he's baffled. Erica's been making her

STEPBROTHER, PLEASE STOP TEASING ME!

stepbrotherly love intentions real fucking clear since the beginning, so...

"Look, how about we play it like this," I say, right as Bella's about to announce the first girl on stage. "We came here to support the girls and we're going to fucking do that. So yeah. We go up together, toss some ones on stage, and don't be a fucking creeper or anything. Except for whatever Olly has planned for Hannah. Let him do that whatever it is because it'll be amusing as hell probably."

"...I know you guys have weird ass ideas about me, but the last thing I was planning was to be a creep..." Olly says, shaking his head, disappointed.

"Sure, whatever, have fun, bud," I say, snickering. "Anyways, are we all in agreement?"

"Sure, but I'm only rooting for Chantel," Chloe points out.

"I'm leaving when Jenny's up," Teddy adds.

"I'm in," Lance says, the only bro out of my actual bros so far.

"I think it'd be nice to support everyone," Amelia says with a nod. "Especially Hannah. I really like playing *Caverns & Dragons* with her at lunch."

"I'm all for enjoying the full stripper experience," Sam says, somehow flirting with people who aren't even sitting with us. Come on, dude.

Amelia fucking eats it up, though. She croons and says how nice that is and... she can't really dance but maybe she can practice something and show it to him in private later? Chloe vehemently agrees, telling Amelia she'll teach her some great clubbing dance moves!

"I'll go up for Little, uh... Chantel, right? And... who the fuck is Jenny again?" Olly asks.

"Cherry Delight," Teddy says with a quick nod.

"Yeah, her. And Roxy, obviously. Fuck, do you know how hot that name is? Goddamn." Olly pauses for a second to appreciate Hannah's stripper name. "But, look, I don't think I can go up and support the cheerleaders. I want Hannah to realize I mean business and I'm not just going up there for everyone, you know?"

"You literally just said you're going up there for half the girls," I remind him. "How is that not basically everyone already?"

"Little Chantel and Cherry Delight are different. That's a supportive thing. If I go up there for the hottie cheerleaders, I think it'll give the wrong impression, you know?"

"For some reason, I understand what you're saying, even if I think you're full of shit."

"Thanks, Jacksy. Knew we were friends for a reason."

Anyways, first up is--

CHARLOTTE

Before we came out of the bathroom, Bella had us pick cards to figure out who was going when. It was just a ten card stack of regular playing cards, hearts only, fanned out and offered to each of us in turn; the Ace of Hearts, then Two through Nine of Hearts, and the Queen of Hearts.

"No Jacks," Bella tells us. "Queens are better, right?" she adds with a wink. "And to make it more interesting, whoever gets the Ace can choose to go first *or* last. Let me know before we head out, though."

Kendra, one of the presumed professional strippers, ended up with the Ace.

"Oh wow," she says, pretending to be excited. "Can you believe it? What an honor. I'll, like, I don't know... go last?"

"Can you please cut the stupid fake amateur bullshit out?" Bella asks her. "I've seen you at so many amateur nights it's ridiculous."

"Have you?" she asks. "Maybe it was someone else?"

Anyways, um... the girl who ended up with the Two of Hearts, who now has to go up first, is:

"Please welcome Cherry Delight to the stage!" Bella calls out.

In hindsight, I think going first is kind of bad? There's a small amount of clapping from most of the crowd as everyone gets used to what's happening and that's about it. I kind of expected more, especially for Jenny. To be fair, the boys are clapping a lot and the romance book club girls are, too. Everyone else is just, um... politely clapping? It's something, at least.

Jenny nods to each of us, trying to look confident. She swallows hard, scoots out of the booth, and heads up on stage to, um... to introduce herself...

We never actually talked about what we were going to say and I know Bella said to play up a fantasy but I don't even know what my fantasy is supposed to be and I'm really unsure if, um... what are the other girls going to say? Oh gosh.

Anyways, Jenny's up. Sorry! I mean Cherry Delight is up...

"Hey, um, hi," she says as she climbs the stage stairs, heading to the front to look out at the audience.

"Louder, honey!" Ruby shouts to her from the middle of the room.

"Sorry!" Jenny squeaks. Then louder, she says, "Um, hi! I'm Cherry Delight. I may sound sweet and innocent, but trust me, boys, I'm not. I, um... I have that perfect mix of cherry sweetness and sensual delight that makes all the boys back at my college go wild. Which, you know, is why there's a bunch of them over there, ready to cheer me on. Hey! Oh, um, there's also this one boy named Teddy that's totally not my brother because that'd be kind of weird and he's going to make an excuse to leave now for reasons entirely unrelated to me but I'm sure he's super supportive and a great guy and--"

"On it!" Ruby says again, giving Jenny a thumbs up and a wink.

"Wait, what?" Jenny asks, confused when Ruby saunters

over to Teddy, taking his hand in hers, and, you know, leads him to the back where the private rooms are.

Teddy, um... he goes? It's really nice of Ruby to offer to help Teddy out because I know how awkward it'd be if he had to sit and watch Jenny perform, even if her outfit is... more on that in a second.

"*Teddy!*" Jenny screeches after him. "What the heck!"

I think everyone assumes this is a comedy skit or something because most of the rest of the people in the club start to laugh.

"Ugh," Jenny grumbles, reluctantly accepting the fact that her brother's going into a private room with yet another stripper. I wonder if they all have favorite songs here? Is that a stripper thing or a regular person thing?

"Ready?" Bella says from the DJ booth, ready to queue up her song.

"Yup!" Jenny says, getting right back into it.

And then--

The intro to one of our favorite pole dancing exercise songs comes on. Oh gosh, I love this one, too! It's really fun to dance to. We have an entire routine for it in class and it's not as pole-heavy as others, but it's a great workout, for sure.

Fabulous by C.U.T. picks up after a short instrumental beginning and Jenny dives right into it.

Also she's wearing the same kind of workout outfit she always wears in class, which is just a pair of black sports leggings with a white stripe going up the outside of each leg, with a matching sports bra and a loose grey sleeveless athletic tank top. The top shows off her midriff slightly, but the sports leggings are high-waisted so it kind of evens out, and the arm holes are extra loose and baggy so you can still see her sports bra a little bit underneath it.

Anyways, um, that's it. That's her stripper outfit for tonight.

The boys and Amelia and some of the romance book club

girls go up to the stage to appreciate Jenny's performance which is really nice. They all have a small pile of bills and, um... they just put a dollar or two each on the edge of the stage. Jenny's busy dancing and doesn't seem to notice. A few other men from the club go up and add more to the pot so, um... yes?

Jenny starts her performance with some flowing freestyle like we usually do, lifting her hands in the air and waving them to the rhythm of the music like a leafy tree dancing in the wind. Once the song picks up from there, she heads into the rest of the routine. Mainly it involves some stomping and pivoting, hip thrusts to move into the beat of the music and emphasize the hip hop-style lyrics. She kicks her foot up and wraps her calf around the pole, reaching higher up with her hands and spinning slightly, using her momentum to twirl to the other side of the stage.

It's, um... it's literally the routine we do in our pole dancing classes down to a T, and she's doing great but also I don't know what to say besides that? I like it a lot and it's one of my favorite dance class songs, though!

"Go Cherry!" I cheer from the special reserved section.

"Babe," Angela says to Clarissa. "Cherry's, like, totally good at this."

"Yay, Jenny!" Clarissa says. "Um, I mean, yay Cherry!"

Also apparently what Jenny lacks in male attention, she more than makes up for in stripper appeal because about thirty seconds into her routine a bunch of them start excitedly dancing around the stage and cheering her on and putting more dollar bills around the edge for her and, um...

"Girl!" one of them says. "This is my *favorite* song to workout to!"

"Love the outfit!" another stripper says. "My exercise outfit looks the same. It's so comfortable."

And, um... I didn't know this before but I guess the routine we do for our pole dancing class is pretty popular in most pole dancing classes because all the strippers who come up to the stage know it quite well and they're carefully recreating the moves Jenny does on the showroom floor without stealing the spotlight away from Miss Cherry Delight.

Bella giggles from the DJ booth and starts her commentary, "In case any of the men are wondering what's going on, this is a popular pole dance class song and, suffice to say, we all love it. Cherry's rockin' it, gentlemen! What a Delight, honey."

Shortly after that, um...

Crystal, the sarcastic stripper I met in the dressing room earlier, runs into the booth with Bella. "Sorry I'm late!" she says. "Here for the commentary, everyone! I'm Bella's co-host and--"

"I don't need a co-host, Crystal," Bella says, glaring at her. "Feel free to let yourself out."

"Aww, what fun would that be, though?" Crystal asks, smirking at her. "Anyways, as for my commentary," she adds, her voice matching the sound of the music. "Cherry's dancing skills are technically fine, but this is a *strip*club, am I right? Lose the clothes, baby girl! At least take off that tank top."

"I, for one, like a little mystery," Bella counters. "I mean, let's be real for a second, clearly Cherry's an attractive girl. Do we need to see everything all at once or can we let ourselves get lost in our imaginations?"

"Bella's a romantic, everyone," Crystal says, giggling. "Unfortunately we all know you shouldn't fall in love with the strippers, so..."

The song finishes shortly after, Jenny ends her routine with a quick climb up the pole and a classic spin that's really fun to do and hard to maintain but I can maybe see how it doesn't look like too much from the outside observer? It's, um... it's just really fun and it's actually a lot harder to do than it looks, though.

Jenny hops down, breathing hard, face red from exertion. She takes a bow, which, um... I don't know if we're supposed to do that but everyone claps and it's fun to watch. Confused as to what to do with the money, she blinks and glances back at Bella.

"It's all yours, baby," Bella says, grinning. "Scoop it up and get your cute little tush back here!"

"Okay!" Jenny says, excited. She kind of ends up getting on her hands and knees to collect her cash which, you know... I can't see it from here but apparently the men sitting up close in the club are enthralled with the view down her shirt.

...They look more excited now than when Jenny was dancing?

Her routine and technique were great, though!

And...

It's at this moment I realize this isn't all about dancing...

I have no idea what I need to do to win the competition, though.

Jenny sits back down next to me, beaming, carefully sorting her tips into a neat pile.

"That was so fun!" she says, excited.

"You were really good," I say, grinning and nodding.

"Like, you were totally amazing, babe, don't get me wrong," Angela says. "But, um... did you forget to strip or what?"

"No?" Jenny says, confused. "Bella said we didn't have to take our clothes off, right?"

"Totally," Clarissa agrees. "And you looked so cute, Cherry! Loved it! Where'd you get that tank top, by the way? I need one for cheer practice, for sure."

"And *this*," Kendra, the pro stripper, says from the end of the reserved section, "is why they call it *amateur* night."

"It's just so easy, though," her friend, Alexis, adds. "I don't want to say it's like taking candy from a baby, but, well... it is?"

"Easiest grand we'll ever make, that's for sure."

"Why are you two even here?" Jenny claps back.

"For the money?" Alexis says, haughty. "Obviously. You and your little girlfriends can pretend and have fun all you want, but in the end you're all just going to be silly little bimbos entering amateur night for a quick fix to impress some boys who probably wouldn't even be interested in you if you weren't half naked. We'll be the ones taking your money and your men home. If we want to, that is. That guy who *wasn't* your brother is pretty cute. What's his name again?"

"Tommy, I think?" Kendra says, cocky. "Mmmm, he *was* cute. Threesome later maybe?"

"His name is *Teddy* and there's no way he would ever--" Jenny starts to say.

"*Bingo!* That's it!" Kendra interrupts, flashing a wicked wink at Jenny. "Let's do it, Alexis. Chat him up later and either take him for all he's worth or take him home to screw with her? Sounds fun."

"Don't even listen to them," I mumble to Jenny. "They're just mean. Teddy would n-never--"

Except then, um...

"Um, excuse you, you old hags!" Angela shrieks. "There's absolutely no way Teddy would *ever* go home with you! And if you try to so much as talk to him, I swear to Jesus I'm going to lose it! Supporting other women only goes so far, bitches!"

"We support the boys, too!" Clarissa agrees. "Especially Teddy!"

"Wait, why especially Teddy, babe?" Angela asks, suspicious.

"Because he's Jenny's brother and she's our friend?"

"Oh, right. Yeah! That's the reason!"

"I'm all for whatever's going on right now," Jenny says. "But can you please support me and Teddy when he's being dragged into private rooms by strippers, too? Just saying."

"Ruby's really nice so I'm sure he's fine!" Clarissa tells her.

"Should I, like, go check on him for you, though?" Angela asks. "Because I'm like totally supportive of you or whatever?"

"Um, he's coming back right now, though?" I point out, literally pointing toward where Teddy is coming back out with Ruby.

"Oh..." Angela says, letting out a puff of disappointment.

Jenny glares at Teddy and gives him the evil eye and Teddy confusedly glares back at her, trying to figure out what he did wrong.

"You know what you did, Teddy!" she shouts at him. "You know!"

"I don't know what you're talking about, Jenny!" Teddy shouts back. "How was your dance?"

"Don't change the subject!" she yells. "It was good, though. Thanks. I had fun!"

"Good! I'm glad!"

The first dance of the night is over now.

I don't know if I feel more or less nervous than when we started, though...

THE GODDESSES OF DESIRE

Episode 170

CHARLOTTE

One of the mid-twenties girls who came with her friend is called up next to dance. They're mostly keeping to themselves but they're nice and talk to the rest of us a little bit now and then. I think they're nervous? I, um... I understand because I'm pretty nervous now too, but...

"Do you want to swap with me?" Alexis, one of the mean girls at the end, asks. "I'm supposed to be third. You're second to last, right? Sometimes it's nice to get it over and done with, you know?"

Which, um... that almost sounds like she's being nice?

"Are we allowed to do that?" the girl asks, blinking over at Bella and Crystal for confirmation.

"You can do what you want," Bella says while the girl's friend introduces herself on stage. "But traditionally the--"

"Alright!" the girl says. To make it official, they swap playing cards, even though I don't think we need them anymore? "Thanks so much. I really--"

"You heard her, right?" Alexis says to Bella and Crystal. "It's a done deal now."

"Why does no one listen to me?" Bella says, shaking her head and sighing. "The early dance spots are usually when the crowd's getting warmed up. The girls that dance later traditionally get more in tips and a better reception. You just traded away your golden ticket. Even if you're bad, you would've made more in tips."

Alexis sits quietly with her friend, Kendra, arms smugly crossed in front of her, grinning and chatting to the other mean girl while now ignoring the pleading look from the other woman.

Before I can say anything, because, um... I'm eighth? That's when I get to dance and I guess it's a good spot? Anyways, Bella shoots me an evil death glare and shakes her head.

"Don't even *think* about it," she says, staring me down.

"S-sorry!" I murmur.

"It's my fault," the woman says. "We thought it'd be fun to come here and do something a little exciting and new, you know? Something different from our boring office jobs. I didn't realize it'd be this cutthroat?"

"It's okay," I say, smiling at her. "Um, I don't think most of us are like that? It's just, um... you know..."

"I can't wait to see your dance!" the woman says, smiling back. "You girls are so supportive of each other. It's really nice."

Her work friend's dance just started so we stop chatting for a little bit and focus on that. She's good, too! I mean, um... not as good as Bella. Bella's *really* good. I bet most of the girls who work here are really good? I kind of want to see them dance too, but I know it's not just about dancing now. There's more to it. There's the, um... the sex appeal and...

...I don't even think I have sex appeal so this is going to be hard...

Right, so, anyways!

The second dance is good. She makes a couple mistakes but she pulls a decent amount of men from the audience and some of the romance book club girls like Joanna and Amanda cheer her on, too. I think part of the reason she slips or stumbles a couple of times is she's nervous, but that's alright. I... think I might also do the same and I hope no one notices or else, um... I don't know, maybe I'll fall on my butt and then crawl off the stage embarrassed? Hopefully not, but I might.

Once she's finished dancing, she scoops up her money in a slightly more ladylike fashion than Jenny did and hurries back to the special reserved section to sit next to her friend.

"You did great!" her friend says, excited.

"That was such a rush!" she says, giggling. "Wow. I think I made the entry fee back, too?"

"That's awesome!" her friend says, smiling ear to ear. And then Bella calls her name and--

"Wait, you're up next?" she asks. "I thought you were almost last?"

"It's almost *too* easy..." Alexis says, snickering from the side, more than loud enough for everyone to hear. "I'll warm them up for you and we'll split the prize like usual, right, Kendra?"

"Yeah," Kendra says, nodding along, ignoring the rest of us. "You won last time so it's my turn tonight."

The woman who traded her spot gives the mean girls a dirty look before heading up to introduce herself and do her dance.

"Are we having fun yet?" Jenny asks, optimistically hopeful. "I counted my tips and I totally made sixty bucks so I'm good. Ten bucks ahead, baby!"

"Babes," Angela says, gritting her teeth. "I know we came to support Charlie and have fun together as a group, but I totally want to beat those mean girl bitches now. *Ugh!*"

"Totally," Clarissa agrees, putting on her game face. It's

kind of like her regular face, but more menacing and less cheerful. "They aren't very nice."

"Like, not even a little!"

"Agreed," Hannah says, nodding along.

"I don't know what you bimbos are getting your stripper thongs in a twist for," Erica snaps back, haughtily tossing her hair over her shoulder and smirking at the cheerleaders. "I'm clearly going to win, get all the prize money, get the most tips, and *then* claim my stupidly hot new sexy stepbro out back in one of the VIP rooms where I'll show him *exactly* what happens there, so..."

"There's cameras back there, by the way," Bella says, off hand. "Seriously, it's not just a song. There's no sex allowed in the champagne room."

"Wait, that's a song?" Clarissa asks, delighted. "Love it!"

"I think she's making things up," Erica huffs. "I've *never* heard of that. In fact--"

"How *old* are you all?" Bella grumbles, annoyed. "Seriously, what the hell? Babies, the lot of you."

"I mean, technically I wouldn't call it a *song*," Crystal adds. "It's more of a comedy skit, but it does have a nice rhythm to it. You could sing it if you wanted to."

"Shut up, Crystal. I don't want to deal with your shit right now."

"Love you to pieces too, Bella!"

"Is, um... is that really a thing or are they making it up?" I ask the other girls quietly.

"I think she made it up but it's kind of funny?" Jenny offers with a shrug.

"I didn't make it up!" Bella gripes. "Once this competition is over, I'm grabbing my phone and showing you."

"Maybe it's like that Ed Sheeran song?" Hannah suggests. "Like, you know, he doesn't think he can find love in a club so he goes to a bar?"

"I thought they called them pubs in England, though?" Clarissa asks, confused. "Is he finding love in America then?"

"If Ed Sheeran wasn't married I'm pretty sure he could find love anywhere he wants, babe," Angela says.

"Seriously, you're all babies," Bella reminds us.

"They have a point about Ed Sheeran though," Crystal says, smirking.

"No, Crystal. They don't. Seriously, don't give them bad ideas."

HUNTER

After Jenny and these two random women do their pole dances, next up is...

"Let's welcome Bastet to the stage, everyone!" Bella calls out as Angela pretends as if she didn't realize she was up next.

The busty blonde cheerleader hops out of the reserved section, eyes wide, mouth open, gasping like she's the recently announced winner of a beauty pageant or something. I don't think this is that kind of place, but I don't know. Do strippers have their own beauty pageants? Maybe that should be a thing. Huh.

Anyways, she hops up on stage and starts her introduction, which, uh... I wish I knew what the hell was going on but I don't.

"Hi hi!" Angela squeals, beyond hyped. "I'm Bastet! Like the Egyptian goddess of kitties and stuff. Which, you know, I totally love them, so cute and cuddly, but when I say *kitty* tonight, I mean..." She makes a not-so-subtle gesture towards her girl parts. The lower ones. Why the fuck am I even explaining this? Holy shit.

"I totally looked it up before I came on stage and Bastet is, like, *also* the goddess of women's secrets, so, like... shhh, don't tell anyone I'm here, alright?" she continues. "It's a secret, boys..."

This is surprisingly effective. Somehow everyone fucking loves it and eats up her act.

"And... like, I'm not saying this is going to happen anytime soon because I'm just a beautiful college girl having some fun, but, like, Bastet? Totally also the goddess of fertility. Which, um... seriously, I'm not having babies anytime soon but until then, practice makes perfect, am I right?"

...Now she has a crowd of ardent followers already circling the stage to toss money at her and I don't even fucking know what the hell this is anymore...

Teddy's no longer sitting with the bros, either. Dammit, Teddy! We need to get him a tracker or something? I'm not saying Teddy's a dog, but seriously, what the fuck, dude?

"Guys, where's--" I start to say.

"Already up there, buddy," Sam says, nodding towards where Teddy's politely sitting next to the stage, waiting to offer Angela some dollar bills.

"Fuck, we're late," I grunt.

"To be fair, I think Teddy's early?" Olly says.

"Maybe..."

I'm seriously trying to keep your secret, Teddy. You're my bro, but come on, you're making this really fucking difficult, you know?

Anyways--

Angela's crowd of dudes is bigger than any of the other girls so far. She nods back to the reserved section, specifically to Clarissa, and quickly shouts out, "Do it just like we talked about, babe!"

Bella starts her commentary before Angela's song plays with, "I have no idea what that means, but please don't."

"Aww, I want to see it, though," Crystal says, pouty.

"No."

And... away we go! Fuck it, I'm ready now. I'm sitting with

Teddy, Olly, who apparently decided to come up even though he said he wouldn't, and Sam. I have my obligatory couple of bucks to shove on stage, and... yeah, I don't know, I really only want to see what Baby Sis has in store but I don't know when she's up, so...

I glance over at her and she smiles back, excited. I kind of want to keep watching her instead of whatever bullshit Angela's about to do, but my stepsister nods to the stage and giggles shyly when I won't stop looking at her, so...

That's not a very good way to get me to cut it out. Probably a great way to make me keep looking at her, to be honest. But, well... eh.

I reluctantly half-focus on whatever Angela's doing, which is:

Nonsense by Sabrina Carpenter starts playing and it seems perfect for the cheerleader because, you know...

Look, nevermind. I'm going to be nice tonight.

Also instead of pole dancing, Angela's performing a cheer routine. Complete with clapping, high V's, and a split. The split kind of works in her favor because with her purple latex skirt she ends up giving her adoring fans a quick panty flash. Except she's not wearing panties, she's wearing her cheerleader bloomers. I'm not about to get into why this is different, because honestly fuck if I know, but it is what it is and that's that.

Then the entire routine takes a turn for the amazing.

"I'm coming, babe!" Clarissa shouts out, which, uh...

Angela spins around fast, heading to the other half of the stage, the one closest to the DJ booth and the reserved section. There's no seating set up there, so no one's sitting there or standing or whatever. Meaning...

"Please don't," Bella says, half-hearted.

Neither Clarissa or Angela heed her warning. Clarissa skips over to the side of the stage while Angela holds her hand out, helping her climb up. They both easily bounce onto the stage together, some practiced and perfect cheerleader bullshit going on. Also, uh... look, I'm trying to stay focused on the technique and supportive bit, but the two of them are wearing matching tube tops and super fucking short latex mini skirts and come the fuck on, their breasts are bouncing every fucking which way and I'm pretty sure they're about to fall out of their tops.

In the meantime, their tips are fucking phenomenal, though. Goddamn.

The horny ass motherfuckers in the club are throwing some serious cash their way. The entire stage is practically covered by money at this point. Angela does a little swish-kick thing to make way for the rest of their cheer routine, which they continue together this time, boobily bouncing up and down, cheerful and bubbly and whatever the fuck else.

"Please feel free to keep the tips coming," Bella says, deadpan. "But I do need to inform Bastet and Desire, who didn't get to introduce herself properly, that they're disqualified. Amateur night is for *single* dancers only."

"Way to spoil the fun," Crystal adds over the speaker system.

"I *told* them not to," Bella points out.

"Did you, though?" Crystal adds. "You said please don't, but..."

"Shut up, Crystal," Bella says, shaking her head.

I also want to add that Angela's mainly been dancing for Teddy this entire time. Like, boobs pointing at him, all her bouncing directed his way, and he's got a clear fucking view of her not-panties every time they flash into view, so...

"Have I supported the cheerleaders enough yet?" Olly asks, trying to covertly glance towards Hannah in the reserved section.

"Probably?" I say with a shrug.

"Out of anyone here, I would've thought you'd appreciate some massive boob bouncing more than the rest of us," Sam says, looking towards Olly like maybe he's got a cold. "You feeling okay, bud?"

"Look, I do," Olly begrudgingly admits. "Like, this is my dream, guys. It *was* my dream. Earlier in the year I'd be fucking stoked. But now, uh... fuck. *Fuck!* Why is life so complicated?"

"It's not really," I point out. "It's a stripclub. Feel free to stare at all the bouncing tits you want."

"Seriously, how are they staying in their tops? I'm completely fucking baffled. It's a goddamn miracle."

"Angela told me they're using body tape," Teddy says with a shrug. "It's like this special double-sided tape you can use so your clothes stay in place?"

"Clever!" Sam says, snickering.

"You just ruined it, Teddy," Olly says, disappointed. "Fuck. I'm going to hang out with Lance. I'll watch the bouncing boobs from back there."

"What a goddamn poet, guys," I say, appreciating Olly's minor alliteration.

"Since they're both disqualified already, should we play the next song right away?" Crystal asks, smirking at Bella from the DJ booth.

"I don't even care anymore," Bella huffs. "Sure, why the hell not?"

In case anyone does care, Clarissa/Desire's song is *Grrrls* by Lizzo, which was apparently a secret because as soon as it starts, Angela watches her cheerleader friend, wide-eyed and eager, gushing on stage.

"Babe!" Angela squeals. "It's, like, totally our song! Oh my gosh!"

"I know, right!" Clarissa says, grabbing Angela's hands and dancing around the stage with her. "When you said we were going to dance together, I totally wanted to pick this one because, like... you're my girl, babe. Always! Love you. Love the rest of my girls, too!" she adds, as both of them turn towards Jenny, Baby Sis, and Hannah. "Love you Cherry, Chantel, and Roxy! *Mwah!*"

Kisses are blown. Girls are loved. Angela and Clarissa probably make like two-hundred dollars in tips between them. They never once get anywhere near the pole, but the cheerleader gimmick is apparently totally a thing that works in a stripclub. Who fucking knew? Huh.

When they're done, instead of taking the stairs down, Angela sashays towards Teddy.

"Hi Teddy," Angela says, blushing and batting her lashes at him. "Did you, like, I don't know, enjoy watching me dance?"

"You were great," Teddy says. "I recognized a lot of the same moves from when you guys are practicing on the sidelines after school."

"I think, like, maybe I got a little *too* into it, though?" Angela says. "Like, um... you could totally see up my skirt, huh?"

"It's a pretty short skirt," Teddy informs her, playing it safe.

Come on, dude...

"Yup! It really is. I think my body tape is coming loose, too. My top might fall off any second. But, like, if it does, you can just totally wrap me up in your big strong arms and hide me from everyone, alright?"

"Uh, sure?" Teddy says. "Do you have more tape? Maybe you could put some on in the bathroom or something?"

"Oh, it's fine!" Angela says, giggly. "I'm, like, pretty sure it'll stay on for a little longer, but, like, let's wait and see, alright? Maybe you can help me out in one of the private rooms later. It's kind of hard to tape everything down by myself, you know? Especially when I'm all wet and sweaty and hot and excited and..."

I think she ran out of words to use because she just sort of stops and resorts to heavily batting her lashes at Teddy who nods along as if her request is completely normal and innocent and not flirty whatsoever.

I'm dying. I'm dead. Teddy, bro...

CHARLOTTE

It's sad that Angela and Clarissa got disqualified, but at least they had fun? I, um... I didn't know what dance they were going to do and I kind of thought they'd rely more on the pole and, you know... they're super pretty so there's that, but going with the cheerleader routine angle was definitely unique. I think everyone really liked their dancing.

"We did it!" Clarissa squeals as soon as they hurry back to their seats. "And, like, wow. That *was* super fun. Huh!"

"I know, right, babe?" Angela says. "We can totally split our tips, too. Let's save it for our roadtrip, alright? Right, babes? We need to do the roadtrip this summer. Like, not right away, but soon! We have a few months before classes start again, so..."

"Y-yes!" I say, excited. "I, um... I'm going to try to save more and..."

"I mean, you'll probably totally win it all and get the grand prize, so you'll have plenty, Chantel," Angela says, somehow playful and yet super serious at the same time.

"I can't wait to see you dance, Chantel!" Clarissa agrees. "Your outfit is super cute."

"It's, um... it..." I mumble, because I haven't really told them all of it and I don't know if I want to, um... oh gosh...

I blink and glance at Bella fast in case there's a sign or a message or something there but Bella's busy announcing the next girl who's supposed to head up and dance, which is--

"Everyone!" Bella says, adorably authoritative. "Please welcome *Roxy* to the stage. I don't get a vote and I'm not supposed to play favorites, but she's one of my top picks for the night, for sure. Please don't do anything weird like the last two, though. Thanks."

Hannah stares wide-eyed at the stage, lips slightly parted, gasping for air.

"I... I don't... g-guys!" she stammers, shrinking low.

Everyone in the club stares at the stage, waiting for the new girl to make her appearance, but Hannah's hiding in her seat, trying to curl up on the floor.

Ummmmm... oh gosh...

This isn't good.

HUNTER

"Everyone, please welcome Roxy to the stage!"

Those are definitely the words my stepsister's stripper friend said, except so far there's no sight of anyone approaching the stage. Also, Roxy's Hannah, so...

"Dude," Olly says, looking from me to the stage to the special reserved section and back again. "This is it.."

"Is it, though?" I ask, dubious.

I don't want to ruin this for him, but, uh... bro, things aren't looking good. Maybe he really did fuck things up on the ride over. Goddamn, Olly.

"What's it?" Teddy asks, joining the conversation.

Not sure that's going to help but I guess it couldn't hurt?

"Olly's about to profess his undying love for Hannah when she gets on stage," I tell him.

"Uhhh, is that a good idea?" Teddy asks.

"No I'm not about to fucking do that," Olly snaps back. "Wait, why isn't it a good idea, Teddy?"

"Look, I don't know how it works for amateur night, but everyone knows you're not supposed to fall in love with the strippers, right?" Teddy says, the voice of reason over here. "I'm actually kind of confused about that rule, though," he adds. "Why aren't we supposed to fall in love with strippers and what happens if we accidentally do?"

Olly stares at Teddy as if he just said the most brilliant and stupidest thing ever all in the same sentence. Which, uh, yeah. I get it, Olly. I do. Teddy's like that. We all know it at this point, but what are you gonna do about it, you know?

"Okay, so," I say to Teddy, hoping to get this out of the way so we can move on. "I don't think anything bad actually happens if you fall in love with a stripper, bud. It's more like a cautionary tale, you know? Like when you tell a little kid not to touch a hot stove because they'll get burned, right? That's this, except we're the kids and the stripper is the stove."

"Oh," Teddy says, nodding along right up until the end. "Wait... so we *aren't* supposed to touch the strippers?"

"I think technically you *can* touch the strippers if they let you?" I say with a shrug. "Buddy, this is my first time in a stripclub, too. Fuck if I know. Why? You know something I don't?"

"Uhh, maybe?" Teddy says, super fucking suspicious.

"Teddy, dude, what the hell?" Olly says, finally coming back to his senses after being dumbfounded earlier. "What stripper did you touch?"

"It's not like that!" Teddy protests. "I mean, it is, but it's not? Guys, stop looking at me like that. Seriously."

Fuck no I won't stop looking at you like this, dude. I stare at Teddy so damn hard my eyes start to hurt. What happened to my poor, sweet, innocent Teddy and which stripper corrupted him?

"Alright, look," Teddy says, jumping into quick storytelling mode. "I was in that private room with Bella and Angela, right? And Bella said it's fine to touch from the waist up while getting a lap dance. So, you know... it's not like I was *trying* to touch anyone, but where do you put your hands?"

"Good question," Olly says, nodding along. "Where *did* you put your hands, Teddy?"

"Keeping them at my side seemed awkward and I couldn't put them in my lap because, you know, it was a lap dance, right? I was trying to help Angela practice, except oddly she didn't use any of her practice lap dance moves when she was on stage so I don't know what happened? Uh, right, so, anyways, I had my hands on her hips at first but she kept moving a lot, because it was a lap dance and I guess that happens? I don't know. She ended up taking my hands and sliding them up and--"

"Got it," I say, interrupting him before he says too much. "It's cool, man. Don't even worry about it. Angela's not a real stripper anyways."

"Does that mean Teddy's allowed to fall in love with her then?" Olly asks, being an asshole.

"I wasn't too worried about Angela but the same thing happened with Bella," Teddy points out, definitely saying way too fucking much. Dammit, Teddy! "Oh, I just realized I'm not in love with Bella though so it's fine?"

"As wonderful as this conversation is, I think we have more important matters to deal with, boys," I inform them, trying to save Teddy from himself.

"Do we?" Olly asks. "I'm pretty invested in whatever the hell is going on in Teddy's life right now and wouldn't mind focusing on that more."

"No," I tell him. "Olly. Take a step back, bro. What were we *just* talking about? It's important. Keep up. Don't lose track of the endgame here, man."

"We were just talking about..." Olly says, taking a second to think it over. "Oh, right! Fuck! Roxy. Uh, Hannah. Whatever. Fuck."

"Whatever happens, just remember to keep your hands above her waist and I think it's fine," Teddy says, offering perfect words of wisdom for our dear friend, Oliver.

"Thanks, Teddy," Olly says. "I appreciate it, bro. Gonna be

hard, though. Fuck. Have you *seen* Hannah's ass? Goddamn..."

I thought dealing with Teddy and Angela was going to be hard enough. Now I have to deal with Olly being a complete fucking idiot over a nerd girl who probably isn't even into him.

I look to Sam for help or whatever, because he's my only sane friend now.

...Or so I thought...

Sam's casually curled up alongside Amelia, who's showing him pictures on her phone, which are apparently of a "not safe for work" variety involving, you know, nubile human ladies and their muscular dragon mates. She's babbling about their roleplaying characters and how they should maybe try to--

I don't even fucking know. I give up after listening to two seconds of whatever the fuck is happening over there. Sam keeps flashing Amelia his patented pretty boy charm, though. Full on sensual smirk, smoldering bedroom eyes, focused on her and only her, tossing out flirty as fuck lines every now and then just for the hell of it.

I have no sane friends now. They've all gone crazy. Someone please send help.

"I'm going up there," Olly says suddenly.

"There's literally no one on stage," I point out.

"I don't care," Olly says, steadfast. "I'm going up and I'm going to show my support whether she decides to dance or not. I need to do this, Jacksy. It's not for her, it's for me. If I don't do it, I'll regret it. I know I will. So..."

"Idiot," I grunt. "Fuck it. Whatever. I'll go with you."

"Cool," Teddy adds. "I'll come. Hannah's my next door neighbor and her and Jenny are friends again so I should probably support her, too."

The three of us swagger up to the empty stage, take our seats when no one else will, and--

ROXY, EVERYONE!

Episode 171

CHARLOTTE

Hannah hides on the floor, mostly out of view from the rest of the club except for us girls sitting in the special reserved section with her. There's, um... there's this small partition in front of our bench and she's huddled behind that. The partition does a pretty good job of hiding our lower bodies, except it doesn't go all the way down to the carpeted floor so I'm pretty sure everyone on the other side can see our feet.

Basically Hannah's hiding behind it but her feet are probably still visible so, um...

I don't know if that's relevant or useful but I'm doing my best to help and that's the only thing I can come up with.

"Can we skip her?" Kendra, the mean girl at the end, says to Bella.

"Clearly she's not going up," her friend, Alexis, adds. "Some of us are here to actually dance, you know?"

Bella glances from me to Hannah and then to the two professional mean girls. "Give her a minute," she says to

153

them. Then, to me, she adds, "Can you deal with her? We can't hold this off forever."

"I... y-yes!" I say, frantic. Umm... I'm going to help my friend and...

I crawl down to the floor with Hannah, sitting my butt on the plush red carpet. It's actually really comfortable for a floor. Huh. I didn't realize how soft it was when I was walking on it before because, um... I don't know if most people who walk on things can tell how soft they are? It's a floor. How many people sit on floors?

...I've probably sat on the floor more often than most people, mostly out of nervousness or anxiety or, um... you know... so I don't know if this is a question I should be asking myself, but...

"Um, hi," I say to Hannah as she cautiously leans low and peeks under the partition as best she can, scanning the feet of the crowd before us.

"Charlotte, I'm an idiot," she says. "I already screwed up on the ride over. What if I go on stage and Olly laughs at me or something?"

"I really don't think he'll laugh at you," I say, hopefully optimistic.

I mean, he seemed interested in her when I talked to him the other day? He could've changed his mind, though. I don't want to tell her either of those things because I told Oliver I wouldn't and, um... if he *did* change his mind and I tell her he's interested in her then I'll feel kind of dumb, you know?

"I guess not," Hannah says, offhand. "He'd probably just ignore me instead. I don't know which is worse, to be honest."

"We're, um, you know... just here to have fun, remember?" I say, trying that and seeing how it goes.

"I know that's what I said earlier, but I still envisioned getting on stage, locking eyes with Olly from across the room, having the most insane and intense visual connection I've ever had with anyone in my entire life, and he'd be so mesmerized just from looking at me that he'd slowly make his way to the stage and I'd, you know, completely seduce him with my rockin' pole dancing skills, just like if I were my character in *Caverns & Dragons*."

"Does your character have pole dancing skills?" I ask, confused.

"Oh, no, not really, but I like to try and seduce people as often as possible, you know? Like, I don't make my character have sex with anyone, but I really flirt it up and get information and sometimes it helps with moving the story along. Tania says we could probably do without my seduction attempts, but come on, what fun would that be?"

"Oh," I say, nodding along, not quite understanding but trying my best. "Um, does it always work, or...?"

"I mean, it's fifty-fifty?" Hannah offers. "...That's a lie. I started keeping track. It works twenty percent of the time and, um... even some of those times it's not that useful?"

"Oh," I say again. I don't have a lot to add here. I don't know if my seduction skills are all that great, either. I feel like I've done okay as far as Hunter goes, but also, you know... he seems incredibly interested in being seduced by me already so I don't know if I have to do much?

I'm not saying it's easy! It's still super hard for me. But I think I could screw up and it'd be okay and he wouldn't laugh at me and it might still work or at least we could try again and have a do-over or, um...

"I see what you're trying to say," Hannah says with a nod.

"You do?" I ask, because I haven't said much and I feel kind of bad about it.

"Even if I fail, it's worth a try, because otherwise I'll never know and I might regret it," Hannah says, headstrong. "Right?"

"...Yes...?" I answer, because that seems like the correct thing to say.

Bella stares down at us on the floor from the DJ booth. I

plead with her with my eyes to, um... a little more time?! I think we can do this if only--

"Is this guy she's talking about your man's friend?" Bella asks, turning her mic off so the words don't blast through the club.

"Um, yes," I say, nodding quick.

"Not Teddy, obviously," Bella adds. "And the other one looks like he's having fun with some other girl."

"That's probably Oliver," I agree.

"He's waiting by the stage for you," Bella informs Hannah. "Get your sexy ass over there before he leaves, Roxy."

"Wait, he's *there?*" Hannah asks, confused. "Already?"

"Yes, he's literally sitting next to the stage waiting for you. Look for yourself if you don't believe me."

Hannah and I peek over the top of the partition. Hunter and Olly are, in fact, sitting next to the main stage now. Teddy's there, too. Jenny's brother looks over and waves to us and I lift my hand and wave back. Olly glances at Teddy to see what he's waving at and, um...

Hannah and Olly lock eyes and I don't know if this is the intense visual connection she was hoping for but maybe?

"Thanks, Charlotte," she says, rising to her feet, standing tall, or at least, well... she's kind of short compared to Olly, but she has a pair of stripper heels on so I think that helps. "I feel a lot better."

"I believe in you!" I tell her, excited. "You can do it, Roxy!"

"Yeah!" Jenny adds, cheering Hannah on. "Go dance your butt off! Just, you know, please don't flirt with my brother again? Seriously, it was super awkward last time and I don't want to be mad at you again."

"I'm not going to flirt with Teddy, thanks!" Hannah huffs, hands on her hips, glaring at Jenny.

"Look, I don't recommend flirting with Olly either because--" Jenny starts to say, and I think she's going to cave and tell her about the dare but then she doesn't.

Hannah marches off, strutting her stuff over to the stage, climbing the stairs with practiced precision, and saucily staring down at Oliver while she prepares to introduce herself as--

HANNAH

Alright, Hannah. You can do this. Seriously, you got this, girl! Nothing bad's going to happen. Even if it does, what's the worst that *could* happen?

...Besides slipping on the pole, falling on your butt, embarrassing yourself in front of the guy you like, and looking incredibly unsexy when the entire point of pole dancing is to look as sexy as possible...

That's, um... that's not going to happen, though! Nope! Not a chance. It's--

I'm trying to do as much positive self talk as I can while I focus on strutting to the stage, climbing the stairs in my low-key stripper shoes, which are really just a pair of round toe cross strap stiletto pumps I bought awhile back to wear in private so I could cosplay as a sexy vampire. I've never told anyone that before, though.

As much as I like to pretend I know what I'm doing when I play roleplaying games with Tania, Amelia, Doris, and Sam, I really don't. The idea of flirting with a boy is a lot easier than actually doing it, you know? Like, in my head I always know what to say and it comes out sounding so sultry and smooth, but also cute and playful, and sometimes a little innocent but hot at the same time? I mean, is that even possible? Who the freak knows!

Anyways, I take a deep breath, standing at the front of the stage, the pole I'm about to dance on right behind me. Oliver is in my peripheral, looking up at me as I prepare to do my thing. I look anywhere but at him because if I look his way I think I'm going to lose it from all the butterflies attempting to buckle my knees and knock me on my butt.

Crushing is *hard*. For real.

Right, so...

"Hey! I'm Roxy!" I say, letting out the words I've practiced for days now. I feel like this part is easier because we do it a lot when we start a new *Caverns & Dragons* campaign, you know? First comes the introductions, and tonight I'm playing the character of Roxy who is--

"Don't let the nose ring fool you," I continue, nervously tugging on the circle of metal that's always dangling between my nostrils. It's small enough not to be too loose like the usual bullring-style, but when I'm anxious I tend to tug at it like that, too. "I'm actually really sweet. Want a taste? Mmm, too bad, boys. I'm waiting for someone special to share my feisty side with. If you think that's you, well... why not come up close and get a good peek at what I have to offer? Seriously though, I'm a princess and a lady and I'll always be that way, but for one special boy in my future, I fully plan on keeping the sugar and turning up the spice when we're alone and in private, so..."

"What did I tell you?" Bella announces from the DJ booth, voice blasting through the speakers. "You're going to have your hands full with this one, gentleman. Or at least one of you will. Which of you will it be, though? Hmmm..."

It's supposed to be Olly but I didn't want to come on too strong. I think I did that on the Uber ride over. I wanted to be flirty and cute and make him super interested and instead I, you know, insulted him by insinuating he comes to stripclubs all the time and has gotten more lap dances than I can count.

I mean, maybe he does? Maybe he has? Maybe he wasn't joking? Freak me, what the heck, Hannah! Stop making yourself even more nervous.

I can't even bear to look Olly's way as I spin around and get ready to start my routine. The music I picked begins to play, *Woman* by Doja Cat, and I quickly unhook the front of my flowing dark apricot skirt, letting it fall to the floor at the base of the pole. It's a whole lot easier to do my moves without the skirt, but I'm also hoping it looks kind of flashy and sexy, you know?

I'm not sure I have much going on otherwise. I'm not exactly busty. I'm not super flat-chested. I'm just... you know, it's enough? Or not.

My matching dark apricot crisscross halter-neck sleeveless top covers the top of my chest entirely, but the way it curves around my, you know, curves? You can see the bottom of my breasts and my entire tummy, kind of like a belly dancer thing going on, which was sort of the point, so...

Under my skirt, the one now laying at the floor by my feet, I'm wearing a similar colored pair of thick panties (and another pair under those just in case), with light beige thigh-high stockings, garterbelts clipping onto a special lace belt looped around my hips just a few inches above the waistband of my underwear. It's way less than I'd wear in pole dancing class, but again, that's kind of the point, right?

I don't plan on staying like this for long. As soon as I finish my routine, I'm putting my skirt back on, scurrying off stage, and hiding with the other girls again until my nerves calm down, but, you know... for now...

Slow and relaxed, enjoying the feeling of my body swinging on the pole as the music lifts and rises, I stay low, feet on the floor while mainly using the pole as a prop to help me swing and slide and dance.

I lift one leg up, hooking it across the pole, spinning sideways, slowly lowering myself all the way to the ground. My hands reach out, as if I'm trying to find the man who will desperately worship my hips and my waist, just like the words in the song. I've been moving on auto-pilot, just going with the flow, the way I know my body can move, sliding whichever way seemed natural and right. I haven't been paying attention to where exactly I'm facing or who I'm reaching out to.

I...

My fingertips are nearly at the edge of the circular stage now. I stretch them out one last time, going for gold, looking up at whoever is in front of me before I pull myself back, up, to continue my routine on the pole.

It's him. Oliver. He stares at me and I stare back at him and I feel like the song stops and it's just us for a second, *this* second, and...

I'm not sure where all the money on stage came from but there's only a few bills in front of him. I blink for a second, because there's, um... there's something else there, too? Oliver smirks and winks as he slowly sides one more piece of this puzzle directly in front of me, right by my fingers.

It's a limited first edition collectible trading card from the *Spellcraft: The Scattering* trading card game I used to play in high school. I still play it now but I'm more into playing *Caverns & Dragons* with the girls because the trading card game scene at college is mostly packed with boys who are a little too elitist and snobby about their nerdy hobby. Girls aren't *real* gamers, at least according to them.

"What the freaking heck," I say, forgetting myself and the fact that I'm in the middle of my pole dancing performance. "Is this real?"

"Yeah," Oliver says, laughing.

"You're tipping me with cards from a trading card game?"

"Alright, so, I'm not trying to be a cheapskate here, but... I was actually thinking more like we could play after if you're into it?"

I need to go. I need to keep dancing or I'll lose my routine and get stuck and have to start all over or, um... realistically I'll just screw up and then make a bunch of stuff up for the end but I really don't want to do that.

I want to finish my dance for him and show him how sexy

I can be, to make the ideas and thoughts and dreams into my head into a reality for once in my life.

...But also this is the most amazing thing that's ever happened to me...

I used to think I wanted to be wined and dined by some aloof, eccentric billionaire who would cater to my every desire and, you know, occasionally tie me up to the bed and have his way with me.

Now I kind of want to play *Spellcraft: The Scattering* with Oliver in a stripclub? At least as long as he keeps smirking and looking at me like that. Maybe we can work our way towards the whole bed-tying, way-having thing at some point too, though? Heck yeah.

"Alright," I say, winking and rolling to the side, flexing my stomach and lifting my upper body while keeping my legs wrapped around the pole.

I pull myself up off the ground and sway and shimmy for a second, letting Olly get a perfect view of my butt just in case I haven't convinced him I'm super interested in him yet. Then I climb the pole a little more, continue my routine, and...

I did it!

I have no idea how but somehow it worked? And the guy I'm into is going to play a nerdy card game based on monsters and magic and fantasy spell battles with me after this so basically tonight's the best night ever.

HUNTER

Hannah's good at dancing and everything, don't get me wrong. She fucking cashed in on her "nerdy hipster girl looking for one guy to go wild with" thing, too. The stage is covered with dollar bills by the end of her dance.

...And then sitting in front of Olly, there's a stack of fantasy-themed trading cards from some nerd game...

"Dude, what the hell?" I say as Hannah scoops up her tips, playfully stealing Olly's cards.

He keeps them in protective plastic sleeves and everything. Not only that, he has more. He has *more*. It's not just the small handful of cards he put on stage, there's, like... I don't even fucking know how many he has but he apparently hid them somewhere and pulled them out for this very occasion, so yeah.

"It was do or die, brother," Olly says, as if we're in the military now or something. "I took a calculated risk and luckily it paid off."

"Whoa, is that a Lightning Squirrel?!" Teddy asks, looking at the top of Olly's deck of fantasy cards.

"Fuck yeah it is!" Olly says, excited. "You play, Teddy?"

"I mean, kind of? I was never that into it, but Hannah used to be super into it and she'd make me and Jenny play with her sometimes. Jenny hated it. Hannah used to play with some people when we were in high school but it was just this club room after school thing that happened every other week or something? I don't know the details. I was too busy with football so I never went."

"Okay, what the fuck is a Lightning Squirrel?" I ask, because I feel like I'm the only regular person here now.

"It's a squirrel that can use lightning magic," Olly says, matter-of-fact. "What the fuck do you think it is, Jacksy?"

"How is that cool, though?" I ask, because seriously, how?

"It's one of the first cards ever printed," Teddy says. "It's just really powerful."

"It's a squirrel, dude."

"Why are you so caught up in the fact that it's a squirrel and not the fact that it can cast lightning spells?" Olly says. "Because, for real, if you met an actual squirrel who could zap you with three-hundred-million volts of pure electric power, pretty sure you'd realize how awesome it really is."

"Why is a squirrel casting spells in the first place?" I counter. "Doesn't make sense."

"I think technically he's made of lightning, too?" Teddy offers. "He's a squirrel made of lightning and he can also zap you with lightning."

"I'm done," I tell them. "I can't have this conversation anymore. I'm sorry. I'm glad the girl's into you, though. Good job."

"Thanks, man," Olly says, snickering. "Little Charlie really bailed me out tonight. I'm glad I asked her for help."

"Wait, you did? When?"

"Fuck, I wasn't supposed to say that."

"Is this that time when you showed up really fucking late to practice and Baby Sis was being weird when I texted her and replying with strange shit?"

"Uh, no?"

"Don't lie to me, jackass."

"I mean, it probably was, but come on! The school year's almost over. It's not a big deal, right?"

"Football practice is life, Oliver. It's life."

"Whatever, man. I still showed up."

I'm just screwing with him now and, uh... we need to get the fuck away from the stage as quickly as possible because Erica's up next and there's no fucking way I'm sitting here while she does whatever the fuck it is she plans on doing. Nope.

Me and the boys head back to our booth and Sam comes over to assist, or whatever the hell he's doing. He takes one look at Olly and his dumb nerd card game and says:

"Whoa! Is that a limited first edition Lightning Squirrel? Nice one, dude."

I stare at Sam and he shrugs as if he's unaware of how weird it is to know this random piece of information. Olly grins and nods back at him and even lets him check the card out. Sam holds it reverently in its protective soft plastic case, admiring the artwork or whatever.

Seriously, it's a squirrel. A squirrel made of lightning.

It does have a fucking badass lightning bolt tail, though. Honestly cool as fuck.

DIRTY DIAMONDS

Episode 172

CHARLOTTE

"Oh my gosh that was amazing!" I squeal as Hannah comes back to the special reserved section after finishing her pole dance routine.

"Like, totally, babe," Angela agrees. "Super hot! Loved when you took off your skirt."

"You're so good, Roxy!" Clarissa says, excited. "Do you dance at stripclubs often?"

Hannah giggles and blushes and shakes her head. "No, but I said something like that to Olly earlier?"

"Does Olly dance at stripclubs often?" Clarissa asks, tilting her head to the side, confused. "Huh! I never would've guessed."

"I seriously hope not," Jenny says, rolling her eyes.

"We shouldn't judge, babe," Angela counters. "I mean, I guess it depends on the stripclub? There's ones for male strippers too, right?"

"I don't think Olly is a male stripper, though?" I point out. "I, um... I think Hannah was saying she asked Olly if he comes to stripclubs often? Not, um... not dancing at them?"

"That," Hannah says, nodding.

"Ohhhhhhhh," Clarissa says, eyes wide with understanding. "Got it! Does he?"

"I don't think so? But he sarcastically said he did so I thought I said something offensive, but..."

Hannah glows, cheeks bright red, eyes so happy, practically gleaming. She holds a bunch of cards in soft plastic sleeves to her chest while she tries to count out the money she made in tips.

"What'd he say to you, by the way?" Jenny asks, casual, trying not to raise suspicion.

"Ohhh, right!" Clarissa squeals. "Truth or Dare! Oh my gosh, I almost forgot about that!"

"Wait, what?" Angela asks. "Did someone tell you all about a Truth or Dare secret thing?"

Her and Teddy and their secret...

"It's... it's not a big deal?" Jenny says, sputtering. "Seriously, can we please not right now?"

"I don't get it?" Hannah says, blinking fast. "What about Truth or Dare?"

"It's, um... it's... n-nothing?" I stammer. "We had a movie night and... Truth or Dare? That's it. That's the story."

I'm kind of hoping that works to defuse whatever situation is about to light up but I don't think Clarissa gets it.

"It was Jenny's dare for Oliver, wasn't it?" Clarissa asks. "After he dared her to show him her--"

"Ohhhh hahaha!" Jenny interrupts, forcing out a fake laugh. "Olly and I talked about that and it's definitely not a big deal!"

"It's not?" Angela asks, also confused. "I mean you showed him your boobs, babe. I thought that's why you..."

"You... you *what?!*" Hannah gasps, glaring hard at Jenny. "Jenny!"

"It didn't even mean anything!" Jenny counters, defensive.

"It was a quick, like, three second thing! Angela and Clarissa were there, too."

"I wasn't there," I say, just in case that helps.

"Wasn't it five seconds, though?" Angela offers, helpful.

"Babe!" Jenny snaps. "Like, for real, you're not helping right now..."

"If it helps, Jenny's boobs are, like, totally goals," Clarissa says, nodding sincerely.

"I can't even believe this," Hannah says, glaring at her not-so-friendly neighbor next door. "After everything with Teddy, you went and did this? Did you *know* I liked him, Jenny?"

"Did I know you liked who?" Jenny asks.

"Oliver! Was this payback for me inviting Teddy over for a sleepover in high school because I thought we were over that and I apologized already, Jenny!"

"Wait, you invited *Teddy* to a sleepover?!" Angela squeaks. "Did he, like... did you two... you know?"

"No, nothing happened," Jenny adds. "Teddy told me because he thought it was a friend thing and I told him it definitely *wasn't* a friend thing and then Hannah and I got in a big fight and to be honest it was kind of petty of me and we recently apologized to each other, so..."

"Except then you showed the guy I like your tits," Hannah points out. "What the heck, Jenny!"

"I didn't even know you liked him! Anyways, he's the one who dared me to do it. What was I supposed to do?"

"Um, *not* do it?"

"Do you even know how Truth or Dare works, Hannah? That's not an option!"

"I mean, it kind of is?" Clarissa says, offhand. "But if you don't do the dare you usually have to do something even worse. We never actually discussed what that would be during our movie night, but I guess we should've?"

"It's not even a big deal, is it?" Jenny says with a shrug. "But seriously, what'd Olly say when you--"

"Show me your boobs," Hannah interrupts.

"Um, excuse you?"

"Look, I don't want to be mad at you and I think this is the only way I can get past it. If Olly saw them, I need to see them, too. Then it's fair."

"That makes *no* sense," Jenny grumbles. "Seriously none."

"You really do have nice boobs, though?" Clarissa says, helpful as always.

"I don't think we should be showing our boobs in front of everyone at the stripclub, though?" I chime in, because seriously, um...

"Technically if there's anywhere we're going to do it, it's here," Angela says, fully on board with the boob showing plan. "And, I mean, it *does* make sense, don't you think?"

"The Cheerleader Guidebook says that if you commit a crime against another babe, even if it's an accidental judgement in error, the babe you committed a crime against is allowed to choose a fair punishment, so... I mean, I'd say it sounds totally fair to me?"

That's Clarissa, our new voice of reason. And, um... I mean, it kind of makes sense?

"That's it then," Angela says, authoritative. If she had a gavel, I think she'd pound it down right now.

"Look, I'm not saying I *won't* show Hannah my boobs," Jenny complains, definitely sounding like a girl who won't show her friend next door her boobs but, um... that's just what it sounds like to me? "But not right now, alright? Like, can we do this later?"

"It has to be tonight, though," Hannah says, stubborn. "I'm supposed to play *Spellcraft: The Scattering* with Olly and I won't be able to enjoy it if I'm mad at you."

"Seriously, what the heck did he say to you when you were on stage?!" Jenny whines. "*Tell me~!*"

"He didn't say anything *yet*..." Hannah says, excited. "But he asked if I wanted to play a card game with him after, and, I mean, I do, right? I do. Yes. Is this a date? I don't know if it's a date. Oh gosh. Guys, am I going on a date?"

"What kind of card game?" Clarissa asks, equally excited. "Is it strip Goldfish?!"

"Babe, first off, it's *Go* Fish, not goldfish," Angela says, correcting her. "Second, shouldn't it be strip poker?"

"I'm really bad at poker, though. I like Goldfish better. Are you sure it's Go Fish? I've always said Goldfish."

"It's Go Fish," I say, agreeing with Angela. "But, um... I guess it doesn't really matter?"

"It kind of sounds the same, huh? Thanks, Charlie!"

Also apparently our silly girl conversation has offended Erica, who keeps glaring at us and huffing and trying to get our attention by glaring at us and huffing. I, um... I finally realize this so I look over and I think she's going to say what's on her mind but instead she just huffs and glares at me.

"Um, hi?" I say to her.

"Don't you *hi* me," she snaps. "You and your idiot friends think this is funny, don't you? Well, it's *not!* Do I need to remind you that this is a competition? Which I'm about to win, by the by. Look, I fully plan on making Huntsy mine before I step off that stage so if you're too embarrassed to go on after me, I understand, alright? When do you want to give up? You can do it before I go up if you want. Then I can, you know, skip the theatrics and just take Huntsy into a back room and let him have his stepbro way with me instead of humiliating you in public like I'm absolutely about to do."

"He's, um... he's not your stepbrother, though?" I point out.

She keeps saying that and I don't understand why because my mom is definitely still married to Hunter's dad and, you know... my dad is still married to Hunter's mom also, so...

"That's what *you* think!" Erica shrieks at me.

"Don't you have your own stepbrother to harass?" Jenny reminds her.

"Who, *Lance?*" Erica asks, rolling her eyes. "He's an idiot. He doesn't even realize what he has right at his fingertips. The amount of times he could've totally defiled my innocence at this point is honestly unreasonable. And how many times has he done it? *None!* He's not my true stepbro. I refuse to accept him as one."

"I'm, like, totally not trying to pass judgement here, but didn't you get expelled for trying to blackmail professors who tried to have sex with you?" Angela claps back. "I don't know what innocence you think you still have that could be defiled, but..."

"That's *different*," Erica says, glaring at the head cheerleader. "Not that *you* would know, you slut."

"That's not a nice thing to say!" Clarissa shouts out. "You take that back!"

"As if!"

"It's fine, babe," Angela says, brushing it off. "Don't take anything she says seriously. She's just mean, like, whatever."

Anyways, um...

"Can you please get on the damn stage already?" Bella informs Erica. "Do whatever Lusty Diamond's gonna do, keep it clean, don't piss me off, and then start all the drama you want, alright?"

"Don't you tell me what to do!" Erica snaps. And then she realizes what she just snapped about and, um... "I *will* get on stage, though. Thanks. And I'm going to show Huntsy exactly what he needs in his life. You're done for, Chantel. If that's even your real name!"

"Um, it's not, though?" I say. "It's... it's my stripper name for t-tonight..."

"*I knew it!* I knew you were trying to trick my poor Huntsy. I bet you aren't even his real stepsis!"

"No, um, I am," I say. I don't know how one is related to the other or how she even came up with that. She's very confusing?

"It doesn't matter. In exactly two minutes and thirty-six seconds, no more and no less, Huntsy will be *mine*... mua ha ha!"

She cackles and struts over to the main stage like she owns the entire stripclub and everyone else is just here for her show, nothing more and nothing less.

"Is she introducing herself?" Crystal asks Bella. "I know the song she picked is two minutes and thirty-six seconds long, but if she's doing an introduction it'll be longer? Or do we start the song as soon as she gets on stage?"

"Shut up, Crystal," Bella snaps. "She's an idiot. Don't listen to her. Nothing she says makes any sense."

"Usually I'd agree, but that outfit... she looks like she's really gunning for it and I'm not sure if any of the guys here will be able to resist if she can actually walk the walk and isn't just talking the talk..."

I nervously glance at Hunter who is looking at me and definitely not at Erica. But, um... she hasn't started dancing yet so maybe that'll change? What if Erica is so good she really can steal him away from me? What if that happens and Hunter doesn't even realize it and... um... and I don't know, but he comes over to me after and says something like:

"Sorry, Baby Sis. I didn't mean for this to happen but you totally aren't my stepsister anymore and I'm madly in love with my ex-girlfriend even if I didn't realize it until now. Her dance completely did it for me. You could never dance like that. You're too shy. I'm going to ask my dad to divorce your mom and my mom to divorce your dad and I'll convince them to marry Erica's mom and dad instead so I can be her true stepbro, just like she wants, and I'll do all the dirty things with her I never could've done with you. Anyways, yeah, sorry. Have a nice life."

...This is my absolute worst nightmare and I don't know what I'm supposed to do except sit here and wait and watch and...

HUNTER

So... that just happened and I really wish it hadn't.

I knew it was coming. This was the entire reason we came to the stripclub in the first place, you know? The stupid as fuck Stepbro Triathlon my self-centered evil ex-girlfriend challenged my stepsister to. Whoever does better in the amateur night contest is the winner of the second triathlon event, right?

Anyways, basically nothing could've prepared me for what Erica had planned for her moment up on stage with the pole so, uh... yeah...

Basically this is what happens:

"Helloooooo!" Erica says, introducing herself. "My name for tonight is Lusty Diamond, but if he plays his cards right, one lucky boy in the audience will be calling me his dirty little stepsister when I'm done. That's right! I'm not afraid to hide it like *some* people I know. I have some hardcore kinky stepbro fantasies that can only be quenched by the most raunchy, rude, crude and lewd, absolutely forbidden, legs weak and bedridden, never hidden, um... I ran out of rhymes, but I think you get it, right? My one true stepbro is in the audience and once I'm done up here he's going to ditch his pretend new girlfriend and drag me away to screw me senseless. Until then, enjoy my show! Oh, and make sure you have your wallets out because I'm more than worth it! Anywho~!"

"Why does this sound like the introduction to a really bad porn?" Crystal asks over the mic before Bella puts Erica's chosen song on.

"Probably because it is?" Bella says, annoyed. "Is it just me or is the stepbrother and stepsister forbidden sex thing really played out? It's not even that bad, is it? I'm sure it depends on the situation and everyone's different, but if your parents happen to marry each other later in life then it's not like you really know the person who's now your stepbrother. There's no history between you and whatever you decide to do at that point is between two consenting adults who may or may not decide to knock boots in bed. I don't get it."

"Spoken like a true stripper," Crystal says, sarcastically clapping. "This has been Bella's Sexy Philosophy Talk, everyone. Thanks for coming out!"

"Whatever, Crystal," Bella grumbles. "You know I'm right."

"You're just so fun to mess with, you half-naked little hottie!"

Bella hits play on Erica's song, blasting it through the sound system for everyone in the club to hear. Erica rushes behind the pole, ready to dance, and... yeah, that's where I kind of zone out because what happens next is dumb as hell and I have no idea what to say.

Long story short, the song is *Gimme* by Sam Smith, featuring Koffee and Jessie Reyez. In case the name of the song wasn't obvious enough, it literally starts with the word "gimme" being said a billion times to the beat of a vaguely old-school reggae track in the background.

While that's happening, Erica does her dance, except calling it a dance is real fucking generous. Instead, she basically shoves her ass out, pushes her chest forward, and stands there shaking her boobs. To be fair, she seems to be doing this to the rhythm of the song, so at least she's got that going for her?

As soon as the next part of the song starts, she stops shaking her stuff and instead gets on her knees in front of the pole. The song slows down considerably at this point, no longer a frantic rush of gimmes flying out of the speakers. My weird ass ex takes this opportunity to pretend the pole in front of her is a dick and she slides up and down, pushing it between her boobs and... look, I literally don't know what the fuck she's wearing but I think what she's doing with the front of her thong and the pole is slightly unhygienic to say the least?

Then the song goes back to gimmes, which I guess is the chorus? I don't even hate the song. It's pretty catchy. But this dance isn't it. It doesn't work. Erica rides the pole faster now, doing the boob thing again except up and down this time. *Bounce bounce bounce.*

I'm not sure what happens after that because I get bored about fifteen seconds in and I spend the rest of the song talking to Sam about my previous life choices.

"You're the one who dated her, dude," he says with a shrug. "I don't know? Why'd you do it?"

"Look, yes, I *did* do that, but we all make shitty decisions sometimes, right? It's my dad's fault. He kept going on about dating hot ass chicks in college and I wanted to make him proud of me or something."

"Aww, buddy," Sam says, smirking. "You don't have to date hot ass chicks. I'm still proud of you."

"Fuck you, man," I say, laughing.

"Charlie's pretty hot, though," he says, winking. "Good job. She's cool."

"This is the only time I'm ever going to allow you to say my stepsister is hot," I tell him. "Never again."

"You excited for her dance or what? Do you know what she's going to do up there?"

"...No..." I begrudgingly admit. "I don't. I'm excited, though. I mean, kind of? Fuck. I'm super conflicted. She's going to be dancing and, uh... yeah..."

"To be fair, I'm pretty sure she's only here for you," Sam points out. "Probably best to enjoy it?"

"I will, but you get it, right? I mean, what if Amelia was dancing on stage? How would you feel about that?"

"No clue. Will have to see when it happens," Sam says, winking. "Might not take long. I think Chloe's gonna drag her up there with one of the strippers by the end of the night."

"Your weird relationship with the nerdy girl who barely stalked you in the past is unhealthy," I say, rolling my eyes at him. "You know that, right?"

"Nah, it's fine," Sam says. "Anyways, she's done now.. You're up, my man."

The song's over. Thankfully Erica's stopped attempting to have simulated sex with a stripper pole, too. Lance politely claps at the edge of the stage because he's way too fucking nice. There's also an oddly large pile of money up there which I guess goes to show that there's a market for simulated sex acts with a stripper pole. Who knew?

"Huntsy!" Erica screeches. "It's okay, baby! You can profess your undying love for me now! I know it's hard, but I'm right here!"

I wince and shove my fingers in my ears because she's way too fucking loud and it hurts my head. "Uh, yeah, gonna pass?" I say.

"I can't hear you!" she says. "What was that?"

"He said he's going to pass!" Lance says, repeating what I said.

I think he's doing it to help but I can understand why she suddenly looks offended...

"He... *what?!*" Erica shrieks. "This is all your fault, Lance! You were supposed to make him jealous. I saw you sitting with him this whole time! Why were you talking to those strippers before? What have I ever done to you to make you treat me like this? You said you had to study but I know that's a lie! I can't believe my mom married your dad! What the hell did I do to deserve *this~~~!?*"

Thankfully she stomps off stage after that whiny tirade and I can go back to hanging out with the boys and, except... wait, shit, no I can't...

"There's always one," Bella says, sighing. "I wish acts like hers weren't as popular as they are, but it takes all sorts and I try not to judge. Can we get back to the real dancing, though?

175

I know sex sells, gentleman, but there's something to be said for *classy,* and, well..."

"I think what Bella's trying to say is we have a classy girl up next," Crystal says, reading between the lines. "Going to be honest, I don't think she can pull this off, though."

"Nobody asked you, Crystal," Bella says, glaring at her.

"Love you too, baby girl!"

"Let's take a quick break for a minute, everyone. I have something to give to my protege. I promise you it'll be worth the wait. Grab a drink while you can, use the bathroom, and get right up next to that stage because once she starts, if you're not there already, you'll wish you were. Let's go!"

I'm fucking there already and I can't wait. For real. Holy shit, I'm excited as hell.

CHARLOTTE

Bella steps down from the DJ booth and pulls me over to a private table hidden slightly behind a red-carpeted column. I nod and sit and watch her intently, hoping for words of wisdom because, um... if this were a movie that's what would happen right about now?

The scrappy underdog that no one expects to take it all is taken under the wing of a jaded, no-nonsense stripper with a heart of gold and through their newfound friendship they, um... win amateur night at the stripclub...

...That sounded a lot more inspirational in my head before I thought it all the way through...

"Look, kid," Bella says, sidling up to me. "I don't know if you can win this. No offense, but those pro girls who keep coming around usually take it. It's easier to win amateur night at another club and bank the thousand bucks than to work an entire night at their own club for half that. But that doesn't mean you're not good or sexy or whatever you're aiming to be tonight. Because you are. You're also a hell of a lot better than whatever I just had to sit through and watch on stage. That's your competition? It was bad. I know you may think it was alright because a bunch of horny assholes threw money at her, but they're only hoping for a lap dance like that after this and, let's be real, we both know it's not happening. But men love their fantasies, so..."

"Oh," I say, nodding along. "Um... I think it's fine if I don't win as long as I do better than Erica?"

"How are we defining *better?*" Bella asks, considering the win condition.

"I... I don't know?" I say, because I hadn't really thought about it until now. I just figured whoever won the competition would be the winner and it'd probably be one of us except there's eight other girls competing so I don't know what happens if one of them wins instead?

Before Bella and I can talk this out, Saskia suddenly appears. She sashays around the carpet-covered red column and slides up to the table like she's done this a million times before. Maybe she has? That would make sense, actually. Also, um...

"I don't know what Bella's said to you, but if I had to guess it's something to do with not worrying if you don't win, right?" Saskia says, sighing and shaking her head at the platinum blonde stripper next to me. "And to that, I say... *never!* What name are we going with tonight, darling? I want to do this properly."

"Um, Chantel?" I say. "It's the name of the heroine in a romance story I'm writing..."

"Perfect!" Saskia says, clapping her hands together once. "Chantel, listen, honey. As the starry-eyed newcomer, no one expects you to win. But we know better, don't we? You have the talent, darling. You have the skill. And if you do what we talked about back at my shop, well... I guarantee you'll take it all home, honey. The money, the man, and best of all, you'll know that not only did you do your best but your best *was* the best."

"Can you please ditch the bullshit inspirational speech?" Bella asks her. "This is amateur night at a stripclub. The clientele here is slightly more upmarket than some of the seedier clubs I've been in, yes. We're not talking about the World Pole Dance Championships, though."

"Wait, are there really World Pole Dance Championships?" I ask. I don't know why that sounds exciting to me because clearly that's not what I'm doing right now, but, um...

"There are, but that wasn't my point," Bella says, laughing. "The point is, just do your best."

"Sure, do that, too, darling," Saskia says, nodding her approval.

"Oh, and wear these," Bella adds.

She reaches under her seat and pulls out a shoebox. It's, um... it's a shoebox so I assume it has shoes in it? She slips it towards me under the table and pops open the top and, um... oh wow...

The most beautiful, sparkling, over the top pair of glittery platform heels I've ever seen in my entire life shine through the shadow of the shoebox, like literal shimmery angels straight from heaven, if, um... angels straight from heaven wore beautiful sparkling over the top glittery platform heels.

They might? I don't know. I've never met one.

Bella carefully lifts the heels from the box and sets them on the floor near my feet. I tug off my shoes and she helps me slide my feet into the clear plastic straps. My feet look so pretty right now. I've never thought my feet looked especially pretty before, but, um... they just really really do right now?

Wow.

"Thank you..." I mumble, staring at my toes.

"I need these back after," Bella says. "I save them for special occasions."

I nod. "Oh, okay, yes."

"Go get 'em, kid," she says, winking at me. "You got this."

"Are you going to do what we talked about?" Saskia asks, excited. "I really hope you are, darling."

"If you don't want to, you don't have to," Bella adds. "It's not a big deal, but... it *would* look amazing..."

"I... I don't know yet?" I tell them, truthful. "I'm nervous."

"It's fine," Saskia and Bella both say. "Whatever you decide, it'll be fine."

On the one hand, I kind of want to because I want to see the look on Hunter's face?

And on the other hand... there's a whole lot of people here...

HUNTER

I'm right fucking here, boys! Let's go!

Teddy's here with me and admittedly I'd usually be kind of annoyed but Teddy's a bro and Angela's doing her best to make him hers so it's cool, I guess. Olly is respectfully sitting this one out, because he's also a bro. Sam's sitting with me but Chloe and Amelia are right next to him so I think that's fine? I don't know.

Chloe is real fucking loud, though.

"Yeah, roomie!" she yells. "Rock it, girl! I want to see you completely freaking dominate that pole like the little bitch it is! Own it, roomie! Yeah!"

"Sam, can you please ask your girl friend to shut up so we can enjoy the show in peace and quiet?" I ask him.

Chloe glares at me like she's going to devour my soul and spit it out in chewed up pieces after and I wouldn't even be surprised.

"No can do, buddy," Sam says, shaking his head. "I have a strict policy of staying out of issues involving two girls, so..."

"I get what you're saying but the issue is between me and

Chloe, even if it seems like it may be between Chloe and Baby Sis, so... dude?"

"Amelia, how much money did you get?" Chloe asks her. "Charlotte will give it back to us after so toss it all on stage for her, alright?"

"I... alright?" Amelia says, confused. "I didn't know how much we needed so I got two-hundred out of the ATM?"

"Holy shitballs, girl!" Chloe says, staring at her, wide-eyed. "I got paid today so I took out my paycheck but I'm only at one-fifty. Seems good, though?"

"Why are your weird ass girls planning on making it rain while my stepsister is pole dancing?" I ask Sam.

"Just enjoy it, my friend," Sam says, wistful. "Just enjoy it."

I mean, I will, but, fuck...

I feel like I need to step up my game and get to the ATM quick except by the time I realize it Baby Sis is heading to the stage and--

CHANTEL'S SECRET

Episode 173

CHARLOTTE

"Ladies and gentlemen, the moment I've personally been waiting for, which means you should definitely be excited if you aren't already--" Bella says, voice projecting through the club as she announces my entrance. "Please welcome Chantel to the stage!"

That's, um... that's me. I'm Chantel now. No longer am I held back by the insecurities and anxiety of being Charlotte Scott. Nope! I'm, um...

This is my way of pretending I'm not super nervous to dance in front of a stripclub showroom full of strangers for the first time ever but it's kind of a lie because, yes, I'm still super nervous and pretending I'm not isn't helping very much. Sorry!

...Also I feel like maybe I should've mentioned to someone before now that I've never walked in heels this high before...

Or, um... just any heels, really. Not even once. Even the shoes the girls got me for my first ever official date with Hunter were barely anything and mostly just regular shoes with the slightest heel, definitely not nine inch platform stripper heels, so...

I step out from my secret hiding spot just behind the column covered in red carpet where Saskia's still sitting, quietly nodding and smiling at me, the highest hopes ever in her eyes as she watches me make my way to the center stage.

I don't get that far, though. I manage a handful of steps alright but I severely underestimated how hard it is to walk on this carpet in very high heels. It's like standing on my tiptoes while trying to walk through thick mud and I kind of sink in slightly and teeter side to side, stumbling forwards, ready to crash into whatever's there but I kind of already closed my eyes in a panic and I'm hoping I don't hurt myself but I'm pretty sure I'm about to and, um... oh no...

My amateur stripper career is pretty much over before it even began?

Luckily I fall into the arms of a stranger except I recognize these arms and they're Hunter's so I open my eyes and he's there, catching me before I disastrously toppled into a pile at his feet.

"Um, hi..." I mumble, batting my eyelashes at him a whole lot.

I just feel like this is a good eyelash batting moment, you know?

"Please stop doing that," Hunter says with a smirk. "Keep it up and I'll drag your ass off before you even get on stage."

"Noooo," I mumble. "I need to dance for you!"

"Maybe take the shoes off?" he offers.

"I, um..."

I consider it for a second because I think maybe he's right but also when I glance over my shoulder I see Bella sitting in the DJ booth and shaking her head at me in that moody, surly way she seems to have down perfectly. I, um... I shoo her off.

...I didn't mean to do that!

But, um, I did and I do and I kind of roll my eyes and

pretend I know what I'm doing and I shoo shoo, waving my hands at her. She stares at me, silently asking me if I really just did that, and I did so I don't know what to say there.

Then she smirks and winks at me.

Oh good. I thought she was going to get mad.

"...I c-can do it," I tell Hunter as he helps me rebalance on these really tall heels.

I think I'm even taller than him with these shoes on and it's kind of neat actually. Who's looking down at who now, buddy?!

...I don't say that out loud because I'm supposed to walk on stage and dance but if I ever learn to walk in very high heels I'm going to do this again and give Hunter a run for his money, let me tell you...

I stumble over to the steps leading up to the pole on the stage and as soon as I make it to steadier ground it's a little easier to walk. Like, um, not a ton easier, but I don't feel like I'm going to fall over at any second so that's good.

"Is this supposed to be sexy?" Erica shouts from the stands. "She can't even walk straight!"

"Hey, shut your goddamn mouth," Bella snaps. "No heckling *anyone* or your ass is getting kicked out of the club. Got it?"

Erica gapes at Bella as if she just told her to, um... I mean, she did, though. She actually told Erica to shut up, so...

"I'm not sure why Bella's been personally waiting for this moment," Crystal adds, co-hosting as best she can. "But the outfit's kind of cute? I mean, it's not what I'd consider a stripper outfit, and it looks more like the kind of thing a party girl would wear to a club, but I'm kind of into it."

"You shut up, too," Bella huffs. "Let the girl introduce herself."

And, um... I think that's my cue. I can do this! I've prepared for this moment. I'm, um...

"H-hello!" I stammer, suddenly realizing this is exactly like that dream everyone seems to have where you're standing in front of a crowd of people and suddenly you realize you're only wearing underwear. Why do strippers do this?! That dream is awful.

"I'm, um... I'm Chantel..." I mumble. And then louder because a nice stripper woman in the back just shouted that she can't hear me and can I speak up a little, honey, I add. "I'm a freelance journalist by day and I've never done anything like this b-before, but I, um... I just got back from visiting a small town in the middle of the woods where I met a stupidly hunky, um... he was a lumberjack? Let's just say, you know... things happened, r-right? And we had to part ways, because I'm a city girl and he's a country bad boy at heart, but... I miss him and, um... this dance is for him! Huntley, if you're out there, I loved our t-time together..."

Bella stares at me again and I think she's about to do her huffy eye rolling thing but instead she just laughs and lets me do my thing.

...I know a lot of the girls went over the top sexy with their character's and stripper names for tonight but I already have a backstory for Chantel in my romance story and I wanted to stick with it, you know?

Right, so, um...

Bella prepares to play the song I picked except it's taking a lot longer than any of the previous songs. She stares at the laptop in front of her that's hooked up to the club's sound system.

After a few seconds of scrunching up her nose and furrowing her brow, she consults with Crystal.

"Do you know what song this is?" Bella asks, pointing to my submission form. "I looked it up and I don't think it's this? Right title, wrong artist."

"The Sweet Little..." Crystal says, reading the words I wrote. "Oh! Bea Miller. Ha! Cute. Your girl got it right, but instead of the entire thing you turn it into an acronym, first letters, like this--"

Crystal types it in for Bella who has a lightbulb moment, eyes wider than I've ever seen them.

"Damn, girl," she says, favoring me with a wicked grin. "Kind of into it, though."

And then, before she hits play, she adds, "Tonight Chantel will be dancing to *S.L.U.T.* by Bea Miller!"

It takes me a second because, um... she spells it out and I'm nervous but then... wait is that the right song? I think it's the wrong one but when she hits play it's definitely the right one, so...

I wrote down:

"That Sweet Little Unforgettable Thing song by Bea Miller please"

Which, it's playing now so that's good.
...Wait, does that stand for S.L.U.T.?
Oh gosh.

HUNTER

My stupidly hot amateur stripper stepsister is working the pole like she fucking owns it and holy fucking shit I'm so hard and so proud right now. It's a seriously conflicting feeling, actually. I never realized a pride-induced erection was a thing before, but here we are, and it definitely is.

Also two of the strippers Baby Sis is up against are pissed off.

"That bitch stole my song!" one of the girls at the end shrieks. "I've been practicing my routine for this song at the club for *weeks*. What the hell!"

"Fuck," her friend says. "What else can you dance to,

Alexis? You can't go up right after her and do the same routine. Unless she sucks at it."

"I mean, she's going to suck at it, Kendra," Alexis says, hairflip over her shoulder and everything. "Look at her outfit? She's definitely not stripping in that."

"Yeah, she can't even--"

The song *just* started and these two are already ruining this for me. I'm trying to focus but, come the fuck on, just shut the hell up over there. Goddamn.

Also shortly after she starts, and I was pretty fucking sure she was doing amazing, Baby Sis stops and waves frantically at Bella to... cut the music?

The music stops. Everyone in the club starts moaning, asking what's going on, why's she stopping? It was just getting good, which I completely fucking agree with, but--

"Um, s-sorry!" Baby Sis shouts to Bella and Crystal. "Can we restart?"

"What's up, baby girl?" Crystal asks. "Did you screw up a move? It's not the end of the world and usually you'd just have to keep going."

"Oh, um, no, it was f-fine..." my stepsister mumbles. "I... I didn't realize the pole was one of those ones that spins on its own, that's all."

"You want it to not spin?" Crystal asks, as if this is a first. "Usually it's easier if it does."

"Ha!" Bella shouts, triumphant. "You know what this means, right?!"

"Um, yes?" Charlotte pretending to be Chantel says.

"No, not you, honey. Saskia! She's doing it!"

"Where's the pin?!" a woman apparently named Saskia demands, leaping forth from behind a pillar covered in carpet.

I have no idea what the fuck is happening or what any of this means but apparently there's a pin and Saskia reverently carries it over to Baby Sis in her palms as if it's a million dollar engagement ring and she's about to propose. I'm completely lost.

Baby Sis takes the pin and awkwardly crawls on her hands and knees to the base of the pole. She pushes it in, *twists twists twists,* doing who the fuck knows what to the pole, and--

"Are you *serious?*" Kendra shrieks. "She's going to dance on a static pole? Good fucking luck, slut!"

"That's why it's *amateur* night," Alexis says, cackling away in the special reserved seating section with her friend. "She probably saw this on some YouTube channel and thinks it's impressive. Which it is, but she'll never be able to--"

"Seriously, if you two don't shut the hell up I'm calling Bruno over to kick you out," Bella informs them.

"As if!" both girls shout, glaring at her.

Bella waits for them to say more to keep her promise and get them booted but they just sit there, arms crossed over their busty chests, glaring.

"Okay ready s-sorry!" Baby Sis says. "Ummm... do I introduce myself again or...?"

"No," Bella says with a sigh. "Song's restarting. Don't stop me again, though. You're done if you try. Hurry up."

"Y-yes ma'am!"

"Call me ma'am again and see what happens, little girl..."

Goddamn, strippers are fucking ruthless, man.

CHARLOTTE

Alright, um... I need the pole to be static instead of spinning because of the friction? It's important for a secret I have planned and I'm super anxious about it so I don't even want to think about it but I hope Hunter really likes it and Bella promised me earlier she'd give me a robe after I finished so...

My song starts again and I hop onto the pole like I

practiced. I just really love the pole dancing part of, you know... pole dancing? Like on the actual pole itself. When we're in class sometimes we do moves next to the pole and then later incorporate the pole with spins, dismounts, and climbs, but I like hanging in the air instead of being on the ground, so...

I'm doing that?

...Also I just now realized it doesn't matter what shoes I'm wearing while I'm in the air because I don't have to balance on nine inch stripper heels this way, so that's a definite win! Yay!

I grab the pole and swing around, pretending I'm a trapeze artist in the circus because that's usually what I pretend when I'm in class. Without the pole spinning on its own, I only make it about three-quarters of the way around via momentum before gravity catches up to me and slows my spin. I keep one hand high and reach the other lower, holding the pole as far apart as my arms can stretch, and flex my tummy, stabilizing myself so I do a sort of, um... I look like a human flag?

I transition quick and do a sort of cartwheel in midair, curling and tucking one leg around the pole while stretching the other out, grabbing my straight knee with my opposite hand and, um... my free hand reaches skywards like I'm waving to the birds.

...This move's called the martini glass and I really love it because I can just kind of spin on the pole while holding myself up like that and it's a whole lot of fun, but also...

This is where the friction part comes in? The song's only just begun but by the end of it...

There's an outfit change? It's easier than saying what actually happens which is, um...

The thinner fabric on the inside of my cutout leggings catches and stretches on the pole as I spin. It takes a few rotations, but finally I feel the *rip* Saskia warned me about.

Basically, um... I usually wear leggings when I pole dance in class, right? And these are like those, except not made for exercising. The cutout parts are pretty bad for pole dancing, actually. They're prone to ripping and tearing and... that's the point, because--

I try not to look at everyone in the crowd because if I do I think I'll lose my nerve. My eyes quickly dart around for one person, though. I see Hunter at my side, staring up at me with literally every expression I could ever want. It's like, oh gosh, really hot, then super eager and passionate, and now a glimmer of lust with a shine of... love, and...

Hunter looks at me like we're going to make love until morning but it's not just going to be soft and sweet. It's going to be hard, demanding, bed-breaking, earth-shattering, but then gentle and desperate, like we can't get enough of each other no matter how close we are and how long we're together. It's like he wants to fill every part of me with every part of him, his heart, his cock, his... his c-cum... and, um... I'm going to squeeze and clench and grip and throb against every single part of him, my body craving all the things only he could ever give me...

In my mind I'm Chantel who had to go home after she and Huntley solved the murder mystery because her time at the log cabin was up but she regrets it and wants to go back even though she doesn't know how, because if she *does*, if she returns, she knows it'll only be for him but she doesn't know if she can do something like that, uproot her entire life for a man she had a not-so-casual fling with during her scant few weeks working on a freelance journalism article.

Except he's here now, he shows up, he sees her dancing and he knows what it means, knows she's doing it for him and only him and she could never do this for anyone else even if there's a million people staring and watching her right here and now, and... but it's only her and him in their eyes and at the end they're both going to *know*. They'll know how they feel for each other and they'll know how they can make it work between them even if they didn't think it was ever possible because they're from drastically different worlds that could never coexist together, not completely, at least.

So, um... that's where I'm at in my head right now as I dance and my clothes slowly start to come undone, the rip I started growing bigger and bigger, cutout leggings unraveling all around me to reveal--

HUNTER

My stepsister is a fucking goddamn beautiful angel of pole dancing perfection and that's all I have to say about that.

Nah, fuck it, I have more. Hold up because I'm going hard over here.

First, the song? Holy shit, it's really cool. It's my first time hearing it so I'm going to paraphrase and say it's about some girl who's happy with herself and who she is and if she's shaking her ass because she likes shaking her ass, and you get offended at that for whatever fucking reason and call her a slut, well, that's on you.

Except instead of saying slut, it insinuates it with the chorus which is perfect for my stepsister because it's, uh... you know, Sweet Little Unforgettable Thing.

I don't know how the girl singing came up with this but it's great. Hell yeah.

Also at first I thought she had a serious wardrobe malfunction issue on her hands, except, nah, Baby Sis knows what she's doing and I'm *here* for it.

At some point during her pole dancing escapades, her cutout leggings that show off the best amount of bare skin, uh... I mean, they get further torn and start to rip away while she's spinning hard on the pole. As if that wasn't enough, she does this climb when she's basically pantless and as she slides down the pole, heading back to the base, moving into a full split on the stage, her bodytight dress slides up her body. She uses the momentum of her downward descent to bare it all basically.

When she's at the bottom again is when the real show starts. Fuck me.

Proud-rection, for real.

Look, I toss all my fucking money on the stage at that point because I'm done pretending I can hold back by only putting a handful of cash up at once. It's just there, a full hundred bucks, and a half second later Chloe and Amelia make it fucking rain, too. Dollar bills scatter through the air and land on stage as Bella and Saskia sneak over and pull either side of Charlotte's completely ripped leggings off, leaving Baby Sis in nothing but a lacy pair of black and pink panties with a shit ton of glitter to match her stupidly hot stripper heels.

No idea how she hid any of this from me but here we fucking are.

In case it's important, because it seriously fucking is to me, she's wearing a black elastic belt thing around her thighs, with garter belts connecting it to the rest of her hot as hell under-outfit which, look...

I'm about to die of blood loss because every fucking ounce is pounding into my cock at the moment.

The dress that stretched up her body when she slid down the pole into a split is almost all the way off now and then it really is all the way off after she tugs it the rest of the way and tosses it at me. That part is both hot and funny because she's doing her best but she gets stuck and awkwardly flails her arms and, come on, I'm trying not to laugh, but, for real, dude.

Right, so, anyways, she's wearing a matching corset and push-up bra that makes her breasts look fucking fantastic and the garter belt action going on below is hooked onto the corset part. The corset curves around her waist and up her torso, just below her breasts, hugging tight, tied in the back with pink silk. Directly above the corset, separate, is a matching bra, everything full of pink lace, black silk, flowers, hearts, and a massive amount of glitter.

Seriously, it's glitter for days over here, goddamn.

Which is apparently the point because as soon as she strips down to her second outfit, Baby Sis climbs the pole again and goes even harder than before.

My stepsister spins and works the pole. She dances like she belongs in the air, performing perfectly, and the only thing I can think about is what it'd be like if she were doing these moves while riding my cock. I think that's kind of the point of stripclub pole dancing but I don't know if she realizes that and honestly she looks like she's having the time of her life so I'm going to save that thought for later and see what she thinks.

Fucking ride me, baby girl...

Also the way she's spinning and going crazy sends glitter scattering every fucking which way. Now it's not just her catching my eye, but a mesmerizing cloud of sparkling glitter that swoops and swirls around her in ways I never realized were possible. Like, you know how glitter gets literally everywhere once it gets loose?

This is that but sexy. It's like she's a goddamn glitter goddess and the silvery white sparkles are hers to command. The shiny bullshit dances across her smooth, bare skin, showcasing her toned curves. Like, come on, I fucking love it, love the fuck out of her, but I also love fucking her, and I'm conflicted on which I should mention when this is over because this is a stripclub and I know we're not supposed to fall in love with the strippers but I already did.

Not even going to apologize for it. I loved her before amateur night even started.

Go fuck yourself, Erica.

Anyways, yeah, I don't know what happened or when it

happened but the girl in front of me, dancing her ass off on the pole, shaking it for all she's worth, doing a phenomenal job of being sexy as hell and so goddamn fucking powerful and amazing, is, you know... *she's mine.*

My Baby Sis. My stepsister. My girlfriend. All mine and no one else's.

The song's done and Charlotte slowly slides down the pole, breathing hard, coming to a soft landing on her knees in a pile of glitter and cash.

And that's when the stripper drama starts.

STRIPPER DRAMA

Episode 174

CHARLOTTE

Saskia struts over to the center stage where I'm currently kneeling on a bunch of dollar bills and glitter. Umm... wow. Huh. It's a lot.

I was a little too wrapped up in making sure I did my pole routine properly and I wasn't paying attention to much else besides that so coming down from my dance-fueled adrenaline high to find myself in a situation I don't fully understand is kind of a weird and exciting rush. Oh, um, I need to give Chloe and Amelia their money back, though. And Hunter! And... I don't know if Teddy put any on stage for me but him too, and Sam and...

My mind is kind of a blur right now and I don't fully realize or recognize what's going on until Saskia clicks up the steps of the stage in her own pair of high heels, drapes a dark black silk robe over my shoulders, and wraps me up tight in it.

"You did great, darling," she says, beaming at me. "You were absolutely wonderful."

"Oh, good," I say. I think I should probably say thanks or, um... mumble that I probably wasn't that good or blush or...

She helps me regain my slightly lost sense of self by urging me to collect my tips. We do that really fast because I need to get off the stage and let the next girl go up, except before Saskia and I so much as walk down the steps there's a very loud commotion going on back in the special reserved section.

"Alexis, I don't know what you want me to do!" Kendra, the really mean professional stripper who wanted to enter the amateur night competition, says to her friend. "That stupid little slut stole my song."

"Just pick something else!" Alexis snaps. "We are *not* losing to a bunch of ignorant wannabe hos. We took the night off to do this and I am *not* going home empty-handed just because you don't have a backup routine. You do this shit every night, bitch. For real!"

"I fucking know that, thanks!" Kendra snaps back. They're both getting louder and louder, drawing more and more attention to themselves. "Look, obviously I could go up and do a half-assed routine but that's not going to win us the prize, now is it?"

"Just fucking *do it*," Alexis snarls, lips curled over her perfect white teeth. "I'll clean up your shitty little mess once you're done and we can talk about this later. Now is *not* the time, Kendra."

Right, so, um...

I pull the robe Saskia gave me tight over my body, tying the silken belt into a bow around my waist. I scurry back to my seat which, um... I have to walk past the mean stripper women and I'm still wearing those high heels and I'm kind of used to it now but not quite so I'm a little wobbly. Saskia helps me stay steady on my feet but the mean girls see me and--

"You think this is funny, you stupid fucking bitch?"

Kendra hisses, glaring at me. "How'd you know what song I was dancing to? Did that dumbass fake blonde whore put you up to it, you slut?"

Her friend, Alexis, huffs, neat eyebrows narrowed hard, staring at me with her arms crossed under her chest, pushing it out like she's going to smack me in the face with her boobs if I get too close. But, um... not in a nice way because I think a lot of men in the stripclub would enjoy that? I wouldn't though, and I'm pretty sure Alexis would do it really rudely to me.

"I... I d-didn't, um..." I mumble, because I really didn't know and if I *had* I would've maybe offered to switch songs or, um...

I don't know because I really like the song I picked and I can see why she's upset because I don't know what I would've done if she'd gone first, either? Probably just danced to the same song, to be honest. I don't know why we can't both choose the same music? Maybe going back to back is a little awkward, but...

"So, that's enough of that," Bella says, no longer in the DJ booth, voice low and harsh. At first I think she's mad at me but then she comes up close and wraps her arm around me, protective, glaring at the mean girls.

"Yeah? What're you gonna do about it?" Alexis asks, smiling sweetly, laughing in Bella's face.

From the DJ booth, Crystal sighs, as if she fully expected this to happen. Bella shoots her a dirty look and a quick grin before raising her hand in the air and snapping her fingers. That's it. No words, just a sharp, loud *snap*.

Nothing happens. Alexis and Kendra start to laugh even louder.

"Is that it?" Kendra asks. "Oh no, you snapped at us!"

"My apologies for the interruption, but we'll get back to the show in a second!" Crystal says into her microphone. "Just taking out the trash, everyone. Nothing to see here."

It takes the women a second but then they realize Crystal means *them*, and, um...

"What'd you call us?!" Alexis shrieks, ready to climb into the booth and fight.

Before she can make it out of her seat, Bruno and another very large man step up. They swiftly pick up Kendra and Alexis, tossing them over their shoulders and carrying them out of the showroom despite their shrieks and kicks and very long nails that look like they could probably do a lot of damage. I feel like the bouncers in the club are used to this for some reason, or at least nothing seems to phase them at the moment.

And then, um...

The trash has been taken out?

"You alright, baby girl?" Bella asks, grinning at me.

"...Yes?" I answer. "That was kind of scary, though."

"Yeah, it happens," Bella says with a shrug. "You did good, though. How was it?"

I'm still a little shaken but...

"Really fun!" I say, excited. "Oh my gosh, thank you for the shoes. They, um... they're hard to walk in but they were fun to dance with. Can I give them back now, though? I think I'm done with heels. I... I'll just wear my own shoes?"

"I get it," Bella says, giggling. "Want to know a secret? I don't like them, either. But they're flashy and fun to wear every now and then. I thought it'd make your night a little more special. Your man sure seemed impressed."

"Did he?" I ask, eyes wide.

Oh gosh, I completely forgot about Hunter. Where is he? Is he mad? I just danced in my sexy underwear in front of an entire stripclub full of people.

I blink and look around and I think Bella knows what I'm thinking because the next thing she says is:

"Maybe give him a private lap dance after we announce

the results of the contest?" she offers with a wink. "My treat. I'll talk to Johnny and let him know to let you two in."

Is... that, um... I mean... sex? In the... there's no sex in the private rooms, though! Also I don't even know how to give a lap dance. It's going to be awkward, isn't it? It's g-going to be...

...Is it strange that I really want to try it, though?

I smile and nod and blush and I still don't see Hunter but I'm back with the girls now and I'm heading to my seat while they look at me like I just did something totally cool and amazing and... just really really great?

There's one person missing from their seat, though. Um, technically three, but I know where Kendra and Alexis went.

Where's Erica?

HUNTER

It takes every fucking ounce of willpower I have to let the bouncers do their job. For real, though. What the fuck is up with those rude ass bitches and why are they shouting at Baby Sis? They don't look like amateurs, that's for sure. Which, you know... it's amateur night so I don't really get why pros would be here, but apparently it doesn't matter because Bruno and another big dude drag their scantily clad asses out of the Paper Slipper and that's that.

Or so I thought, except--

One person decided to take advantage of the distraction and, look... I don't know why but my ex-girlfriend is suddenly no longer sitting with the other girls who entered the amateur night contest and instead she's standing in front of me, smiling in the most wickedly sweet way imaginable.

She looks like a little kid who thinks they got away with something bad, except literally just looking at her gives it up. I don't know what she did yet, though? And that's kind of a huge fucking problem because whatever it was I'm pretty sure it was really bad. That's the kind of person she is.

"Huntsy!" Erica says, waving to me with her fingers, just waggling those motherfuckers my way. "I just, you know, came over to say hi. I mean, look, my sweet little sugar stepbro, after watching Chantel or Charlotte or whatever her *real* name is do her cute little dance, I can see why you might think she's, like... acceptable. Clearly she's *not* and I'm the only stepsis for you, which I'm going to prove to you shortly, whether you like it or not. That sounds like a threat, doesn't it? Hehe! It's not, I promise! Well, anywho, I'm sure *Chartel* won't like it much, but it's not personal, you know? The world of stupidly hot and forbidden love is too hardcore and cutthroat for most people. Like, if you can't handle that amount of heat, stay out of the bedroom, am I right?"

"Aren't you supposed to be over there?" I ask, jerking my head towards the seat she's definitely supposed to be sitting in. "Can you go away, please?"

"You're *so* funny, Huntsy!" Erica says, giggling maniacally. "Or should I start calling you stepbro now? It's inevitable, don't you think? You're going to be mine, especially after I'm done with her once and for all, so..."

What the fuck is she talking about? For real. I have no idea. I'm so fucking confused and--

I glance over at Lance to see if he knows except the dude's studying. He's got his two textbooks and he's going hard reading one of them. He took a break to sit by the stage for Erica's sake, because, uh... I don't even fucking know, man. He's nice enough but the dude's kind of weird? Tell Erica to fuck off, bro. Seriously.

Anyways, what happens next is Erica looks very very hard at one of Lance's textbooks. I don't think she realizes I can see this, or maybe she doesn't think it matters? To be fair, I don't think it matters at first but then she casually reaches out for the book and Lance just kind of shrugs and nods at her

200

and I feel like something's happening but I don't know what yet and--

"Thanks so much for holding onto this for me," Erica says, smiling sweetly at her actual stepbrother. "You aren't as useless as I thought!"

"Uh, thanks?" Lance says. "I mean, you asked me to bring it so you could study with me after the contest was over, right? It's actually really nice when you think about it. You've never wanted to study with me before. I remember you asked me to study one time when we first met after our parents got married but then you had to take a shower and you left the bathroom door wide open while I was sitting on your bed. But then we never studied, so..."

"Please! Do *not* remind me," Erica says, gritting her teeth. "What kind of stepbro *does* that, Lance? I made it *so* obvious. I don't know how it could've been any *more* obvious. All you had to do was walk right in while I was naked and wet and have your forbidden way with me, but *NOOOOO!* What is *wrong* with you?!"

"We'd only just met?" Lance answers, absolutely baffled. "I didn't know you that well. I don't know if it's normal for us to be taking showers together, either? I don't have any other brothers and sisters, and I guess I've never asked anyone what they do. If we wear our bathing suits maybe it's fine? Kind of hard to shower properly that way, though."

"You absolute moron!" Erica screeches at him. "No. No no no no no! You don't wear *anything*. You get naked, you storm into the bathroom like you know what you're doing, you get into the shower whether I like it or not, you spin me around, slam me against the wall, and you make me beg you to stop while you do anything but! How stupid can you be?!"

"That sounds like assault?" Lance says, head cocked to the side.

"Agreed," I say, just because I'm sitting right next to the dude and I feel bad for him. "That's definitely a crime."

"I know, right?"

"*THIS IS WHY YOU'RE NOT MY REAL STEPBRO, LANCE!*" Erica shrieks, way too fucking loud.

Literally everyone in the club can hear her and if most people weren't focused on the fact that two bouncers just dragged some strippers out of the club I think it'd be super fucking awkward.

Erica slams her hand on one of Lance's textbooks, wraps her fingers around the spine, and starts to snatch it away. I don't know if now's the time to study, but maybe she's finally giving up on the Stepbro Triathlon thing. I mean, she clearly already lost, so yeah.

The textbook is for a really fucking weird class, though. The book's entirely brown with a faux leather look, like it's old and ancient or something? I don't get it. It's a textbook.

Printed on the front in all capital letters is the title:

BETRAYAL 101: A BRIEF HISTORY OF BLACKMAIL, DECEIT, AND TREACHERY

What kind of fucked up class is that? Lance, bro, I totally get it now. Weird shit's going down, dude.

Erica smirks at me, snapping the textbook away, shoving it against her chest, finally covering her goddamn boobs. She turns to walk away and as she does I see a flickering red light on the spine of the textbook, the side that was previously facing the center stage.

Something clicks in my head. I don't know what. It's bad, though. This is it. This is the reason. This is why my ex walked over here with that look on her face.

Before I can say anything, a girl wearing a white blouse and black pencil skirt with glasses casually strolls up to Erica, digs her fingers into the spine of the book, and forcefully tears it away. Erica spins, gaping and gasping, snatching out to grab her book back.

"Excuse you, that's *mine*," she shouts. "What do you think you're--"

Natalie, the cheerleader's legal advisor, who, uh... I mean, whatever, dude. I have no idea why, but she's here. Fuck it. There's probably a reason. She always has a reason.

Anyways, Natalie holds the textbook just out of Erica's reach, twists sideways to keep her from stealing it back, and then turns the book on its side, pages facing up. She scans cover for something or other, seems to find what she's looking for tucked into one side of the spine, flips and clicks a button, which is weird as fuck because it's a goddamn textbook, and--

The entire thing pops open like a box. Which, you know, apparently it is? It's one of those secret compartment hidden book things with the pages carved out in the center. A small handheld video camera fits into the hidden compartment, the lens pushed into a hole in the spine, which is apparently what the red flashing light from before was.

...My evil ex-girlfriend planted a hidden camera in a textbook, asked Lance to bring it to the stripclub, and recorded my stepsister dancing half naked on a pole...

Holy fucking shit, how insane can a person be?

I mean, as far as Erica goes I already know the answer, but come the fuck on, this is way worse than anything she's ever done before. I think it is, at least. Who the fuck knows, man?

"Thank you very much," Natalie says, neatly removing the video camera and popping it into her purse. She briefly considers what to do with the book and eventually opts for tossing it in a nearby trashcan.

Erica stares at her the whole time, face burning progressively more and more red, angry as fuck.

"How *dare* you!" Erica wails, some demonic fucking demon sounding bullshit streaming from her mouth. "Who do you think you *are?!*"

Panicked, Lance looks over at me and Sam and Olly and Teddy and, you know... just all the guys.

"Guys, I didn't know," he says, low, hurt. "Seriously, I thought she wanted to study. I... fuck, I'm so sorry. I just..."

"Dude," I say to him. "You're kind of slow sometimes, but it's cool. I get it."

"No, seriously, I feel really bad," Lance says. "If I'd known that's what she was doing I never would've done it, but I guess I did, even if it was on accident. I don't know what to do."

"I think saying sorry is enough," Teddy tells him.

"It's not your fault, man," Sam agrees. "I mean, you probably should've expected she was up to something, but..."

"Look, I'm all for railing on Lance and making him beg for forgiveness," Olly adds, shifty-eyed. "But first, is anyone else wondering what exactly's on the camera? I'm not saying we shouldn't destroy it later, but if I could have some alone time with it to, you know... rewatch Hannah's performance in private so I can, you know, evaluate her beautifully artistic and creative dance moves..."

"You need to get laid," I tell him. "Holy fucking shit."

"Dude, I'm fucking trying, but I'm also trying to be moderately respectful about it, you know?"

"Is it respectful to jerk off to your future girlfriend's pole dancing routine?" Sam asks, and, winking, he adds, "Asking for a friend!"

"We all know Jacksy would do it," Olly counters. "Don't even lie, either. You loved Little Charlie's performance."

"Guys, it's one thing to masturbate to porn," Teddy informs us. "But we need to be respectful of the girls, too."

"Yeah, exactly," I say, fully in agreement with Teddy. "Which is why I would *ask* Baby Sis if I could jerk off while watching a recording of her dancing on a pole, and not only that I'd offer to do it in front of her, because that's the polite thing to do."

"Uh, that's not what I meant but I think if you ask her first it's fine?" Teddy says, conflicted. "This is getting weird."

"Alright, can we compromise then?" Olly asks. "Hold onto the tape until I know if I have an actual chance with Hannah and *then* I can ask her if I can jerk off while watching it and I'll even see if she wants to join me? Fair?"

"As wonderfully enlightening as this conversation is," Natalie says, smirking and rolling her eyes at us. "And, trust me, I really do enjoy a good mutual masturbation session. But, no. I'm confiscating this recording and it will be disposed of as soon as possible. Sorry, boys. I have the cheerleaders' reputation to uphold. I'm sure you understand."

I mean, I do. But also, fuck. Charlotte's pole dancing performance was hot as hell and I feel like this is a one-time only opportunity, so...

Also apparently a bunch of the working strippers sitting nearby heard our entire conversation, realize what happened, and...

"Bella!" Ruby shouts. "This chick broke the No Pictures rule!"

Bella's ears perk up and she hones in on what Ruby just said, immediately finding the source of her objection. Which, you know, it's Erica, who's currently having a major meltdown temper tantrum, stomping her feet like a child on the red carpeted floor.

"On it," Bella says, nodding to Ruby.

Bruno and the other big dude are busy but apparently there's a lot of big dudes working at the Paper Slipper just in case of emergencies. They're really efficient and prepared here.

"How *dare* you!" Erica shrieks as a muscular man in a dark suit easily drags her out of the main showroom. "You can't do this! Huntsy, I'll be back! Wait for me, baby! It's only ever been you! I promise!"

And then she's gone so thankfully I don't have to deal with her anymore. Baby Sis stares at me from the special reserved section, head tilted to the side, lips slightly pouty and pursed. And, yeah... I'll explain everything to her soon but apparently it's not the end of amateur night yet, so...

"Guys... thank you for letting me hang out with you," Lance says, awkwardly reaching for his textbook, rushing to get up and leave. "But I think it's probably a good idea for me to go now? Seriously, I'm so sorry about Erica. I don't know what she was thinking and she just kind of does this sometimes and I feel like I should know by now and I'm trying my best to understand her and be a good stepbrother but it's harder than I thought, you know?"

"Dude, you really don't have to leave," Olly says, sighing. "I was just screwing with you before. You're fine. It's not your fault."

"Yeah, I just... I mean, I think I should, though," he says, swallowing hard.

"It's cool," I say to him. "Do what you have to do, bro."

"Thanks," Lance says with a sigh. "Sorry again. But thanks for everything. And, uh... yeah..."

He gets up to leave except his stripper friends from earlier see him as easy prey again or something and descend on him en masse as soon as he's away from the pack. Which I guess is us. I don't know why they waited for him to be alone, but apparently Bella told them our group was off limits and they're really good at sticking to the rules. Strippers, man. They're so wholesome and respectable as fuck. I appreciate them.

Not sure if Lance does but the dude's smothered in boobs on all sides and dragged to a private booth to be swooned over by attractive women so I don't know what else to say there. I think he'll be fine.

"I... what, no?" Lance says, confused.

"Let me help you study, baby!" Gia says, sultry. "I *really* want to help you relax when you need a break. You're just so cute, Lance! I can't handle it."

"He's not just yours, Gia," another stripper says with a

perfect pout. "We can help him relax together. It'll be better that way, won't it, baby?"

"I *guess*," Gia says with a flirty shrug. "I mean, if Lance is fine with it, I am, too..."

"I mean, I do have more studying to do?" Lance says, conflicted. "Actually, I could really use a coffee if that's alright?"

"Aww, I love that," Gia says, fawning. "I'll get you one, alright? Do you have cash or your card, baby? Do you want to open a tab?"

"Card, I guess?" Lance says. "Just, uh... nothing expensive, please? I'm kind of on a budget."

"It's alright, honey," Gia says, taking Lance's debit card when he pulls it out of his wallet. "You have to save your money for the special things in life, right? Did you know there's a two for one discount on lap dances tonight?"

"No?"

"There is! And we love giving discounts to cute guys like you, so..."

"Uh, okay?"

"Perfect! Be right back with your coffee, baby."

Good luck and godspeed, Lance.

While that's happening, Bella gets back into the DJ booth once more, ready to announce the final results of Amateur Night at the Paper Slipper...

Can't get enough of Charlotte and Hunter's story?
Keep reading right away!
Stepbrother, Please Stop Teasing Me! (Volume Fourteen)

A NOTE FROM MIA

Make sure you don't miss any of my new releases by signing up for my VIP readers list!
Cherrylily.com/Mia

Hey there!

The Amateur Night competition is here and it's going hard! Instead of just making this one a competition on its own, I thought it'd be more fun to treat it like the girls having a night out, haha. They seem to be having fun so far, don't you think?

I also wanted to flesh out the potentially budding relationship between Olly and Hannah, and to hint at more going on between Angela and Teddy. How will those couples work out? We'll find out in future volumes, for sure.

I just really like the side characters and thought it'd be fun to give them some of their own screen time too, you know? It makes their moments with Hunter and Charlotte more interesting and also gives everyone more fun moments together.

One thing that I really wanted to focus on when I started writing this story is that Charlotte's changing for herself instead of being pushed to change completely by others. The cheerleaders like her for who she is and are always happy to offer advice or help when needed, some of which is a little crazy but fun in its own way. And Hunter has always been into her even if he teases her a lot. Instead of telling her to do things a certain way, Bella's been attempting to get Charlotte to use her natural appeal to win at the stripclub competition. And so on and so forth!

I just think the story's more fun that way. Charlotte's evolving on her own and going to people for help when she needs it, and she's trying new things and discovering everything that she likes and wants to do. She'll always have the help of her friends, but they'll never push her too far or make her too uncomfortable, you know? Just a little discomfort every now and then when she's up for it, haha.

Which, you know... apparently led to her deciding to dance in a stripclub for everyone. The sky's the limit, apparently!

Seriously I really don't think she thought this one through, but she's doing great so far.

And... a private room lap dance for Hunter soon? That's coming up next!

We're also heading into summer break, finishing off the last Stepbro Triathlon challenge, which will be different and interesting, and giving Hunter and Charlotte a break as they head off to Las Vegas for that trip their parents offered them.

There's going to be so much to look forward to in the next volume. You're seriously going to love it so much! (The private lap dance scene is one of my favorites, for sure.)

If you're enjoying Hunter and Charlotte's story, I'd love love love if you could leave a review! It's always a nice extra thing to do and I appreciate them so much.

How did you like Hunter's creative thinking for the

Valentine's Day special? What about Charlotte's night at the stripclub so far? How are you enjoying the side stories with their friends, too?

Thanks so much for reading Stepbrother, Please Stop Teasing Me! I can't wait to show you more!

~Mia ^_^

ABOUT THE AUTHOR

Mia loves to have fun in all aspects of her life. Whether she's out enjoying the beautiful weather or spending time at home reading a book, a smile is never far from her face. She's prone to random bouts of laughter at nothing in particular except for whatever idea amuses her at any given moment.

Sometimes you just need to enjoy life, right?

She loves to read, dance, cuddle with her cat, and explore outdoors. Coffee and bubble baths are two of her favorite things. Flowers are especially nice, and she could get lost in a garden if it's big enough and no one's around to remind her that there are other things to do.

She comes from New England, where the weather is beautiful and the autumn colors are amazing.

You can find the rest of her books (here) or email her any time at mia@cherrylily.com if you have questions, comments, or if you just want to say hi!

ALSO BY MIA CLARK

Stepbrother With Benefits 1

"Friends with benefits, stepbrother with benefits, what's the difference?"

"Um, we're not even friends, Ethan?"

Rule #1 - It's only supposed to last for a week…

Daddy Issues

Good girls get cuddled. Bad girls get spanked…

Keep it up and you're mine, Fiona. Forever.

A Thousand Second Chances 1

Gavin Knight has a secret he can't tell anyone…

He's reliving the same day over and over again.

Trapped in a time loop? Might as well be a bad boy, right?

It's going great up until he meets Everly Adams, the only girl who's stuck in the same situation, and remembers *everything*…

Milton Keynes UK
Ingram Content Group UK Ltd.
UKHW020936201123
432908UK00022B/3300

9 798890 370129